CAPTIVE EVER AFTER

JULIA SYKES

CHAPTER 1
SAMANTHA

This wasn't the first time I'd paced back and forth across my opulent bathroom for five agonizingly long minutes, but that didn't mean the waiting became any easier with experience. Guilt nipped at me, adding to my anxiety. I really shouldn't be sneaking around Andrés like this, but I had to know. And I didn't want to get his hopes up again just to disappoint him.

We'd been trying to get pregnant for almost a year now, but my tests kept coming up negative. My periods had always been irregular, so Andrés wouldn't necessarily suspect that I might be pregnant this time. I'd asked our housekeeper to buy extra tests for me, and she'd promised not to tell my husband. It wasn't exactly as though I could make a covert trip to the drug store and buy some for myself. Our private island didn't have a Walgreens.

I wanted a baby with Andrés more than anything, but right now would be really bad timing. Like, the worst.

No matter what the result, I wouldn't tell him I'd taken another test. If it was negative, he didn't need that disappointment on his emotional plate at the moment. And if it was positive...

I couldn't stand the tension any longer. I'd been pacing along the far side of the massive bathroom, tracking an invisible path from the jacuzzi tub to the huge shower stall. Now, I rushed across the tiled floor to the double sinks, my gaze fixing on the little white stick.

All the air whooshed out of my chest. Two pink lines. Not one.

I'm pregnant.

I braced my hands on the marble-topped counter to support my trembling frame. Joy rushed through me, fizzing along the pathways of my veins to flood my system. A giddy, delighted laugh bubbled up from my chest before I could hold in the ecstatic sound.

A sharp knock on the door made me jolt with a yelp. My guilt rose in a wave, diminishing my happiness.

Shit.

How the hell was I going to keep this secret from Andrés?

"Are you okay, *sirenita?*" His deep, rumbling voice drifted through the closed door.

"I'm fine," I promised, my voice catching. I cleared

my throat and tried again. "Just about to take a quick shower."

"Do you want some company?"

"No!" I took a breath. "No," I said, more calmly. "I'll be right out. Ten minutes."

I stifled a groan. Why hadn't I said I was taking an hour-long bubble bath? Now, I only had ten minutes to get my shit together and pretend like my world hadn't just changed forever.

I couldn't hear his footsteps retreating, and I suspected he was still outside the bathroom door. Knowing my husband, he'd just break the lock and come barging in if he thought I was distressed for some reason. I loved his fierce protective streak, but that could prove problematic today. It was going to be hard enough arguing my case without him knowing I was carrying his child.

I pressed my palm against my belly, but I didn't dare linger by the sink. I rushed to the shower and turned on the water. Andrés must have decided to leave me to it, because he didn't smash down the door to check on me.

I stepped under the hot spray and drew in several deep breaths, willing my fingers to stop shaking. Moving on auto-pilot, I washed my hair and quickly shaved my legs. I needed to feel and smell normal to Andrés, or I might rouse his suspicions. He was almost unnervingly perceptive. Probably because he focused on me so obsessively. He would keep track of my heartbeat at all times, if he were able to.

Usually, I didn't mind his obsession. I was equally enamored with him, even if my devotion didn't manifest itself in the same way as his controlling behavior. But that was why we worked as a couple. He needed to dominate me to express the depth of his love, and I needed to submit to him. In my absolute surrender, I proved that I loved him enough to give him anything he asked of me. He might have the upper hand in our power exchange, but our relationship was symbiotic. We were partners in life.

I would definitely need to leverage all my willpower to remind him of that today.

I straightened my shoulders and turned off the shower, bracing myself for the argument we were about to have. It took less than two minutes to dry off and run a brush through my wet hair. At the last second, I hid the evidence that could ruin all my plans; I stuffed the pregnancy test into an empty tampon box and secured the lid closed before tossing it into the trash. There wouldn't be any reason for Andrés to go snooping through the garbage.

Satisfied that I'd successfully covered my tracks, I slipped into one of my silky black robes and stepped out of the bathroom. I padded through the house on bare feet, looking for my husband.

I found him in the bedroom, his massive body taking up nearly half of our king size bed. Every mouth-watering inch of him was on display. His thick cock jerked in response to my sudden presence, and his tanned skin practically glowed in the tropical sunlight that streamed through the huge windows. They provided a stunning view of the pristine beach, but I wasn't at all distracted by the picturesque scene outside.

He stretched, his corded muscles rippling and flexing. My lips parted, my full attention fixating on his powerful physique. I didn't notice the scars that marred his chest and abdomen, or the wicked furrow that had been carved into his cheek. He was utterly perfect, and he was all mine.

A low sound of approval rumbled from his chest. "You look hungry, *gatita*." His voice dripped with arrogant amusement, and his scar twisted around a smirk.

Damn it. Busted.

I licked my lips and forced myself to maintain eye contact.

Don't look at his cock. Don't look at his cock.

His dark gaze swept down my body, admiring me at his leisure. "Take off the robe," he commanded.

My fingers fisted in the silky material, and I instinctively drew it closer around my body, willing it to protect me like armor.

His smirk dropped to a frown. That fearsome expression had brought many men to their knees, and my own threatened to buckle in supplication.

I locked up my joints, standing straight and holding my ground. "I need to talk to you."

His eyes narrowed, and he slowly got to his feet, moving with the controlled grace of a predator. He stalked toward me. "That was an order, *cosita*," he said, an edge of warning in his soft tone.

I swallowed hard and took a step back. "This is important," I insisted breathlessly. Even as trepidation made my heart flutter in my chest, my sex pulsed in response to his erotic threat. I had to stay focused, or Andrés would obliterate all of my rational thoughts with carnal lust.

It was more imperative than ever that I keep my wits about me.

He didn't stop advancing on me until a mere inch separated us. I could feel his body heat pulsing against me, his aura of power teasing across my pebbled flesh. For a few seconds, he simply stared down at me, pinning me in place with his sharp black gaze. When he finally lifted his hand and trailed his calloused fingertips down the line of my vulnerable artery, I was practically quivering with need, desperate for his demanding, puni-tive touch. My pulse jumped beneath his fingers, and he cocked his head at me, studying me with open curiosity.

"My little pet is nervous," he drawled. "Did you do something naughty, *gatita*?"

"I think I found Valentina." The words tumbled from my lips. I hadn't wanted to tell him so abruptly, but this truth was better than revealing the results of my secret pregnancy test.

The incisive spark vanished from his eyes, and the harsh lines of his face went slack. His hand stilled on my throat, his thumb resting on my artery while his fingers curved around my nape. His entire body tensed, his hand flexing against my neck.

I'd seen Andrés driven to the edge of madness with rage before, but I'd never seen this... I wasn't sure how to put his expression into words. His mind seemed to have shut down, his shock as visceral as though I'd stabbed him through the heart.

Fear fluttered in my belly. My anxious explanation began to spill out of me in a frenetic stream.

"I mean, I'm almost positive it's your sister. A 'Valentina Moreno' appeared online this morning. I've had a search constantly running to ping me if her name comes up. So, it did. She just appeared out of nowhere. It was on an order placed with a florist in California. The payment wasn't in her name, but they noted Valentina Moreno in their system for pickup. So obviously, I checked who paid for it. The card they ran belongs to Adrián Rodríguez. And I remembered you told me that your brother, Cristian, sold Valentina to Vicente Rodríguez when she was fourteen. There wasn't any online trace of Valentina Moreno after that."

I gasped in a breath and continued babbling, very aware of Andrés' hand on my throat. "I did more digging on Vicente and his associates. I couldn't find anything on your sister, but starting a few months ago, there are traces of a 'Valentina Sanchez.' I hacked some email accounts and found out that her husband, Hugo Sanchez, was looking for her because she'd been, um, taken by Adrián Rodríguez." I didn't want to say

7

abducted. The implications of Valentina's story were already horrific enough without painting an ugly verbal picture for Andrés.

"So anyway, it looks like the order placed with the florist in Los Angeles is for a wedding. It looks like Hugo Sanchez disappeared, and now she's, um, well... Valentina is marrying Adrián Rodríguez. Vicente's son. And, yeah. That's it. I have some footage of her that I grabbed from some traffic cams around the florist shop. I thought maybe you could take a look and make sure it's her? I mean, I'm pretty sure it is, but you should probably check. Before you do anything, um, drastic. Like, we should be sure. You know? I mean——"

My unrelenting stream of words abruptly ended when Andrés' big hand shifted from my throat to cover my mouth. Something finally flickered in his eyes, and his gaze focused on my face.

"Breathe," he ordered.

I drew in air through my nose, and oxygen rushed to my head. I realized I'd barely paused to breathe in my anxious babbling. The resultant rush made my brain buzz, and I grasped at Andrés' strong shoulders for balance. His arm closed around my lower back, the iron band supporting me and drawing me closer to his body. He released my mouth and eased his long fingers into my hair, petting me in the way that always calmed both of us.

I let out a shuddering sigh and pressed my cheek against his hard chest. His hand curved around the back of my head to trap me there. I didn't want any space between us, and he clearly didn't, either. I could feel his heart thundering against his ribcage, and he drew in a deep breath to center himself.

After several seconds, he seemed to master his emotions. His heartbeat slowed to its normal, reassuring rhythm, and his grip on my body eased to a gentler hold. His warm breath ruffled my hair as he pressed a tender kiss on the top of my head.

"Show me," he murmured. "I need to see the footage."

"Okay," I agreed. "It's on my laptop."

He allowed me to extricate myself from his embrace, and I noted that he slipped on a pair of boxers while I walked across our bedroom to retrieve my laptop. When I returned to him, he'd settled his bulky frame on the edge of the bed. He patted the mattress, indicating that I should sit next to him. I complied, pressing my body so close to his side that I might has well have been molded to him. He needed my support right now, and I craved his nearness. What I was about to show him could lead us down a dangerous path.

I swallowed my worry for his safety and opened my laptop, clicking on the file I'd saved for his inspection. The video filled my screen. Since I'd pulled it from a traffic cam, it had been recorded at a distance from the woman. I'd zoomed and enhanced her image as much as I was able.

I already knew the woman was Andrés' sister; all the

information I'd uncovered pointed to that fact. If I hadn't been basically ninety-nine percent certain, I wouldn't have presented him with the possibility that I'd found his beloved Valentina. Beyond her bronze skin and thick, wavy black hair, there weren't many physical similarities between the half-siblings. Her face was drawn in fragile lines, whereas Andrés looked as though he was carved out of granite. There was a hint of commonality in their high, defined cheekbones, but her eyes were obscured by stylish sunglasses.

Andrés stared at the video in silence for a moment. Then, he reached out and trailed his fingertips along my screen, as though he could reach through it and touch his long-lost sister for the first time in over fifteen years. I looked up to study his features. His jaw ticked, and he swallowed hard. His dark eyes were over-bright, and he blinked quickly to suppress tears.

I pressed my palm against his scarred face, directing his gaze to me. "It's okay to be emotional," I said gently. "It's her, isn't it?"

"Yes," he replied thickly. "It's Valentina." His hand left the screen, and he buried his fingers in my hair. "You found her," he rasped. A single tear spilled down his cheek. I brushed it away with my thumb.

"What are we going to do?" I urged softly, knowing he'd want to act immediately. We had to formulate a plan to rescue his sister. If I didn't start discussing it calmly and rationally now, he might descend into a mindless, vengeful rage and rush headlong into a dangerous situation. I'd done my research on Adrián Rodríguez, and the powerful drug lord was notoriously sadistic and lethal.

I suppressed a shudder at the idea of Andrés' sister being trapped with a man like that. Andrés didn't need me to show any hint of weakness or worry at the moment. Now, my job as his partner was to get him through this without it blowing up in our faces. I wanted my husband to get his sister back, but not at the cost of his safety.

"So," I began when he didn't respond immediately. "I already found a suitable mercenary group we could contact for tactical support."

When Andrés and I had retired to our private island to live our lives in peace, he'd abandoned his criminal empire, and I'd ensured that my friends at the FBI could locate and arrest all of his former associates. Andrés no longer commanded a small army of ruthless killers, but that wasn't what we needed right now, anyway.

Well, we needed men, but not an army and definitely not killers. I wanted to rescue Valentina, but I wouldn't allow Andrés to blacken his soul with more blood on his hands.

"We can do a simple extraction," I continued. "We just need a handful of men to back us up when we go in to get Valentina."

Andrés' dark brows immediately drew together, casting forbidding shadows over his onyx eyes. "*We?*" he repeated, clearly ready to quash the idea of me accompanying him to LA.

I lifted my chin and summoned up my bravado. "Yes, *we*. You need me on the ground with you. We're doing this the smart, safe way. There won't be a firefight, and you won't be storming Rodríguez's complex. That would be stupid, and we're not stupid. Besides, do you want to risk Valentina getting caught in the crossfire?"

His lips thinned, his scar drawing deep on a scowl. "You can work remotely from here."

"You know I'll be more effective if I'm close by. It'll be faster and easier to adapt to changing circumstances. If there's a freaking ocean between us, I can't back you up."

His fingers tightened in my hair, lighting up my scalp with a little twinge of warning pain. "I don't want you anywhere near Rodríguez."

I stared directly into his eyes, my will clashing with his. "Well, I don't want *you* anywhere near him, either. But I know you won't agree to send in the mercenary team without taking part in the op yourself. If you're going, I'm going."

"This isn't up for discussion, *cosita*," he growled.

I poked him hard in the chest. "You're right. It's not up for discussion, because I'm going with you and that's that. End of discussion."

He tugged my head back sharply, exposing my

throat. "I could just chain you to our bed and leave you here."

"But you won't." My defiant declaration came out a bit more tremulously than I would have liked, but I doubled down. "You respect me too much to do that to me."

His jaw worked as he ground his teeth in frustration. He knew I'd effectively ended the argument.

"You're too clever for me, Samantha," he said tightly.

I offered him a lopsided smile. "Checkmate."

"I never should have taught you how to play chess," he muttered.

"Probably not," I agreed. "Oh, and one more thing. Promise me you won't kill anyone, okay?"

His face hardened to stone. "When it comes to Adrián Rodríguez, I'm not making any promises."

CHAPTER 2
ANDRÉS

Thank god Samantha's not pregnant, I thought for the dozenth time since we'd left the little safe haven on our private island. A week ago, I couldn't have imagined the thought crossing my mind. I wanted a child with the woman I loved more than anything, but ever since Samantha had told me she'd found Valentina—and backed me into a corner about taking her on the op with me—I'd become relieved that my wife wasn't pregnant.

As it was, my possessive instincts when it came to Samantha were an itch beneath my skin, a burning sensation in my gut. It took all my willpower to honor my promise and not chain her to our bed to keep her well away from danger. If anyone dared to threaten her during our mission, I wouldn't be able to suppress my violent urges. She'd managed to tame the monster in me, but I was almost frightened to contemplate what I would become if any harm came to her.

I'd agreed to her stipulation that I arm the mercenaries we'd hired with tranquilizer guns rather than carrying the real firepower I'd prefer. Samantha thought I was a good man at my core, and I tried to be better for her, to be worthy of her. But she would never truly understand the sadistic impulses that had been etched into my soul. Knowing that I was going to extract Valentina without mutilating anyone set my teeth on edge. The urge to punish every man who kept her in captivity was nearly overwhelming. If it weren't for Samantha's fierce insistence that I rein myself in, I would have cut a bloody path through my sister's captors.

That course of action might assuage a fraction of the guilt that plagued me. The loathing that I directed at myself for failing to protect Valentina could be unleashed on the men who'd hurt her. I wouldn't be fully cleansed by washing my hands in their blood, but it would feel good for a few fleeting minutes as they suffered and died.

Other than myself, there was one man who ultimately deserved to be punished for Valentina's grim fate: my brother, Cristian. I wished I could kill him again. More slowly this time.

My hands curled to fists at my sides as I fantasized about crushing his windpipe and watching him gasp for mercy as the light left his eyes.

"Andrés?" Samantha's gentle, soothing voice called me back to reality. Her slender fingers stroked my forearm, easing the violent tension in my muscles. I turned my full attention on her and found myself captured by her steady aquamarine stare. "Everything's going to be okay," she told me with the weight of an oath. "We're going to get your sister back. She'll be safe, and you'll protect her."

"What if I can't?" I asked on a quiet rasp before I could bite back my anxious words. I'd failed to protect Valentina all those years ago. I'd let Vicente Rodríguez carry her out of our home. I'd been too weak, too soft to fight Cristian. I'd watched them take my sister as I laid in agony on the hardwood floor of our living room, curling up in a cowardly attempt to protect myself from Cristian's beating.

Samantha cupped my cheek in her hand, threading her fingers through my hair to call me back to her. I might own her, but she possessed power over me that I'd never granted to another person. Only she could master the beast inside me.

"You can," she swore. "I know you'd do anything it takes to protect Valentina. We're not going to leave her with Adrián Rodríguez one more day. We're going to get her out, take her home with us, and no one will ever find her. I'll make sure of that. You know I can cover our tracks better than anyone. No one will hurt her ever again."

A shudder ran through my body as unbidden

thoughts of what had probably been done to my little sister raced through my mind. I knew what men like Rodríguez were capable of. I knew what *I* was capable of, and I didn't delude myself that Valentina's captors possessed the shadow of a moral code I'd lived by before I met Samantha. I'd been perfectly content to train women to please me sexually, but I'd never taken a woman who didn't beg me to fuck her. Somehow, I'd convinced myself that rape was the line in the sand I wouldn't cross.

"Everything's going to be okay," Samantha promised again, commanding my attention. "We're almost in position. Then, I can scramble cell reception around campus and loop the security cams in the area. Rodríguez will never be able to track us. He won't even know who took her."

My clever pet had quickly formulated our plan to extract Valentina. Once Samantha discovered that my sister had been going by the surname Sanchez, it had taken mere minutes for her to discover that Valentina had recently enrolled at UCLA. My wife had wasted no time hacking into school records to get Valentina's class schedule, and we'd mapped out exactly where and when she'd be coming out of her lecture today.

Samantha would wait in the safety of our armored SUV at the edge of campus while I went in to retrieve my sister. The mercenaries we'd hired should already be in position, taking out the half-dozen men that Rodríguez had assigned to the area in order to ensure

Valentina had eyes on her at all times. With Samantha scrambling cell service and blocking Wi-Fi for the few minutes it would take me to get to Valentina, no one would be able to call Rodríguez for backup, even if any of my sister's captors managed to evade the surprise assault of our mercenary crew.

Samantha had taken the extra precaution of assigning us false documents to get our small team into the US without arousing suspicion. We'd taken our private jet from our island to LA, but all connections to my name had to be thoroughly scrubbed from our flight pattern. My pet might still be in contact with her friends at the FBI, but we both knew they'd try to rescue her from me if they flagged me entering the country.

No one would take Samantha from me. I'd kill anyone who tried.

The SUV came to a stop. "We're here," Samantha said, still maintaining a gentle tone. Her softness helped calm me and prevented me from succumbing to the rage that simmered just beneath my skin. "Let's do this. Let's get your sister back."

My fingers sank into her copper hair, and I twisted the fiery strands around my fist to forcibly tip her head back. Her pupils dilated, the incandescent blue of her irises narrowing. Her pretty pink lips parted on a soft gasp, her body reacting to my control instantly. I kept her locked in place, imposing my will on her.

"Do not leave the car under any circumstances," I

commanded. "Davis is armed with real bullets." I tipped my head at the mercenary I'd hired to man the vehicle and keep Samantha safe while I went in to rescue Valentina. "If anyone comes near you, he will kill them."

"Andrés—"

I placed my hand over her mouth, smothering her protest. "I swore to you that I won't kill anyone unnecessarily, and I will honor that promise. But I won't risk you. Stay in the car. No matter what. Do you understand?"

She nodded as much as she was able with my grip on her hair. Satisfied that she would comply, I eased my hold and trailed my fingers through her silken locks. The feel of her softness beneath my harsh hands kept me grounded. She trusted me completely. I had to trust in her, as well. Samantha wasn't stupid, and she wouldn't put herself at risk.

Suddenly, she pressed her palm against the back of my neck, dragging me toward her so she could crush her lips to mine. She poured her strength into the kiss; my kitten was fierce despite her physical frailty. I returned her aggression with ferocity of my own, taking her lower lip between my teeth in a sharp warning. She would obey me and stay in the safety of the SUV with Davis armed and guarding her, while she protected all of us. I might be rescuing Valentina and ensuring Samantha's safety with the threat of violence, but her formidable mind would allow us to get through our op without being detected, and she'd help us vanish without a trace. In a matter of a few minutes, I'd have my sister in this car, and we'd all be on our way back to the airport.

Samantha pushed at my chest, and I allowed her to break the kiss. "You have to go," she urged, slightly breathless. "I'll be right here when you get back."

I nodded my agreement and released her. She immediately grabbed her laptop and opened it, resting it on her thighs. Her fingers began to fly over the keyboard, and I trusted that she had the situation well in hand.

"Okay, we're good," she announced. "Security cams on campus are set up on a loop. I'll handle the traffic cams as we drive to the airport. Cell reception and Wi-Fi are out now, too. We have eight minutes. Go get your sister."

I wanted to linger, to tell her how she awed me with her bravery and intelligence. But there would be time for that later. The clock was officially counting down, and I had to get to Valentina.

I got out of the car, making sure I heard the click of the locks before I strode away. The vehicle was secure.

I hurried away from the SUV, my movements slightly jerky. It felt unnatural to put distance between Samantha and myself when we were surrounded by potential enemies.

I pulled the baseball cap I was wearing farther down to obscure my features, tipping my chin toward the ground. The security cameras might not be recording any footage of me, but my scarred face was difficult to hide. If anyone stopped to look at me, they'd remember the monster they saw prowling across their campus. I didn't want any reports getting back to Rodríguez that might suggest I was the one who'd rescued Valentina. We were going to disappear, and he wouldn't have a hope of stealing her back from me.

I tried to keep my stride purposeful but not noticeably rushed. The three minutes it took to reach the lecture hall seemed to drag on for hours, and by the time I stopped outside the building's entrance, my heart pounded against my ribcage as though I'd sprinted from the car.

Right on time, the doors opened, and coeds began streaming out of the building, transitioning between classes. My heart leapt up into my throat as my eyes searched the crowd.

The sunlight caught on her shiny black hair, and her skin glowed bronze beneath its summer glare. The face I remembered from my childhood, that had haunted my nightmares for over a decade, was different now. Her cheeks were hollower, her delicate features defined more sharply than when she'd been a round-faced young girl.

My feet closed the distance between us before I could formulate any thought about approaching her.

"Valentina." Her name left my lips on a hoarse rasp. Something burned deep in my chest, and my heart expanded in my throat, cutting off my ability to speak.

She blinked away the sunlight in her eyes and

focused on me. Her thick, dark lashes flew wide, her jaw dropping on a gasp. She recoiled from me.

Pain knifed through my gut, and my hand shot out to grab her upper arm, preventing her from putting distance between us. I'd longed for this reunion half my life. I couldn't bear to lose her for even a moment more.

She jerked against my hold, her dark chocolate eyes wide. I recognized the frenzied light in them. I'd seen it all too often in my lifetime.

Valentina was terrified. Her gaze fixed on my scarred cheek. She didn't recognize me as her brother; she only saw the mangled beast Cristian had made me.

My muscles flexed, my fingers digging deeper into her arm. She winced and stilled. My stomach twisted as I recognized the quick capitulation of a woman who fears violence from men.

"Let me go," she demanded, her voice low but holding an edge of steel I hadn't expected.

"I can't." My grip tightened, as though I could bring my sister back to me by force. "You have to come with me."

"I'm not going anywhere with you." She tried to twist away.

I yanked her closer.

Fuck. My emotions surged, wreaking havoc on rational thought processes. I knew I was scaring her, but I couldn't find the words to explain myself. I'd recognized her instantly, but she didn't know me. The years hadn't been kind to me, and my horrific appearance went deeper than the furrow carved into my face. I was crueler than the teenage brother who'd been her best friend. I hardly saw anything of that boy in myself anymore. Valentina was looking at the monster I'd become, not her beloved big brother.

I deserved her revulsion. I'd failed her. I hadn't protected her when she needed me most.

I shook my head sharply, as though I could physically rid myself of the roiling emotions that fogged my mind. We didn't have time for me to succumb to my self-loathing. The seconds were ticking down, and we had to get back to the SUV before cell service was restored. Samantha could only scramble the signal for so long before we attracted too much attention due to the anomaly.

I forced myself to ease my hold on Valentina's arm, but my fingers remained iron bands, shackling her to me as I began to walk toward our getaway car.

She walked along with me, matching my pace so I didn't increase the strength of my grip. Still, her words dripped with venomous warning. "You're making a big mistake. Leave me alone, or you're going to die."

"I'm not leaving you," I vowed through gritted teeth. "Never again."

She remained silent for the space of three paces. I could feel the sharpness of her incisive gaze slicing at my skin like Cristian's knife. She was staring at my scarred cheek, my ruined face. Of course she wouldn't recognize me. I had to get her back to the car, back to

Samantha. My clever pet was smarter than me. She was better than me; the superhero I could never be. She'd be able to explain everything to Valentina. I couldn't seem to string two thoughts together, much less coherent sentences.

"Andrés," Valentina's soft voice whispered over my scarred flesh, and a shudder ran through my body.

I didn't pause to look down at her, even though I craved to see the recognition in her eyes. All I could do was keep walking. We were running out of time, and if I faced her now, I wasn't certain how I'd react. All I was certain of was that hesitating now would put all of us in danger. I wouldn't allow Rodríguez time to realize something was wrong. I had to get Valentina out of LA.

"Andrés, wait," Valentina implored. "You have to let me go. Just stop and listen to me. Adrián will kill you if—"

My muscles seized as rage slammed into me. I froze in my tracks and rounded on my sister. "He will never hurt you again," I swore on a snarl. "I'm taking you somewhere safe."

She clutched at my shoulders, holding on to me with desperate strength. "I am safe. Adrián loves me. He would never hurt me. But he'll kill you if he thinks you're trying to take me away from him. Please, listen to me. If his men see you touching me, they'll shoot you before I can explain."

"There's nothing to explain," I growled. "I'm your brother, and I'm going to protect you. I know I failed you, but I won't now. Never again. Rodríguez's men won't shoot me. I've taken care of them. But we only have a couple more minutes. Samantha is covering our tracks, but we have to go."

"Who's Samantha? And what did you do to Adrián's men? He won't like it if you've killed them, Andrés. You have to let me call him and explain before this gets out of control."

"Samantha is my wife." My entire body practically vibrated with the need to get back to her. I'd left her alone for too long, and if Rodríguez realized I was trying to take Valentina, Samantha would be in danger. "We have to get to the car."

I started walking again, and Valentina stumbled along beside me. "I can't leave with you," she said, anxiety straining her tone. "Please, let me call Adrián. We can sort this all out."

"I won't negotiate with the man who's holding you hostage," I snapped.

"He's not holding me hostage. I love him, Andrés. I want to be with him."

"No." I dismissed the idea immediately. "You don't."

She dug in her heels, refusing to budge another step. She straightened her spine and lifted her chin. I caught a flash of the headstrong girl who had been my best friend when I was a boy.

"Yes, I do," she replied bluntly. "Adrián saved me. I'm with him willingly. I love him, and I'm marrying him tomorrow. Now, please. Let me call him and explain what's going on before he tries to kill you."

I stared down at her, my brain struggling to comprehend what she was saying. For so many years, I'd loathed Vicente Rodríguez. Ever since Samantha had told me Valentina was marrying his son, Adrián, I'd focused that hatred on him. He was my enemy, a threat to my little sister that should be eliminated.

"Andrés," she said my name again, speaking in a low, rational tone I often heard from Samantha when I was being particularly mercurial. "I want you to meet the man I love. I won't lose you again. You're my family, but Adrián is my family, too. I'm not going to allow you to kill one another over a misunderstanding."

I bit out a curse. "We have to get back to the car."

Her dark eyes narrowed. "Did you not hear anything I just said? I can't leave with you, big brother."

"I heard you," I replied grimly. "But you're not going to be able to call Rodríguez until we get to Samantha. She's made sure that cell service is down in the area while I came in to get you."

Valentina started walking more briskly. "We'd better get to her before Adrián's men realize I'm with you, then. They will shoot you if they see us together."

"They won't be a problem. I already had my team handle it."

She sighed. "Adrián's going to be really pissed at you for killing his men. I've dreamed about finding you and us all being together as a family, but this isn't how I imagined things would go."

"You've been looking for me, too?"

"Adrián's been helping me. He told me Cristian is dead that that you disappeared about a year ago. I didn't know if you were even alive, but I hoped..." She trailed off and swallowed hard. "I don't have time to get emotional right now. Let's just get to Samantha, and we can work everything out back at the house."

"Agreed. I don't think Rodríguez will be too mad, though. Samantha insisted I arm my team with tranq guns. She wouldn't let me kill anyone."

"Good. That's good. He's going to start freaking out if I don't call him in the next few minutes. He usually gets updates as soon as I leave campus. He can get very... Well, he worries about me."

My gut reaction to the implication that Rodríguez was a controlling, possessive bastard was to grab Valentina and put an ocean between them. But my sister claimed to love him, despite what Samantha had discovered about the man's ruthless reputation.

I supposed my own reputation for brutality wasn't all that different from Adrián's. And I most certainly would slaughter anyone who tried to take Samantha away from me. If it weren't for the fact that we were completely isolated and safe on our private island, I probably would have her watched at all times, too. In fact, I probably wouldn't let her out of my sight at all.

I released some of my violent tension on a resigned sigh. "I understand," I conceded.

I understood all too well. That didn't mean I was happy about the situation. I didn't want my little sister to marry a man like me. She deserved better.

CHAPTER 3
SAMANTHA

J amming cell reception and disabling Wi-Fi in a ten-block radius was super easy. Like, so easy it was almost kind of boring and a little anticlimactic. Even though I was no longer an active FBI agent, I still spent my days digging through the deep web, following leads, and connecting dots. That was a process, a pursuit; a puzzle to solve. This was just...a party trick. Literally, I scrambled the frequencies in a matter of seconds with a few keystrokes. Looping the security cameras on campus was also ridiculously simple.

Now that Andrés had gone to get Valentina, there wasn't much for me to do other than try not to become consumed by my anxiety for his safety. I knew the mercenary team we hired had already done their job quickly and cleanly. Davis—the man who was currently sitting the front seat, waiting to drive us back to the airport once we extracted Valentina—was connected to the rest of his team via wireless comm units. They'd all confirmed that Rodríguez's guards around the lecture hall had been neutralized.

I stared at the data on my screen, as though obsessively monitoring it would somehow get Andrés back to me unharmed. I'd done everything I could to ensure the path to rescue his sister was safe. All I could do now was wait at my laptop to reassure myself that everything was going smoothly.

Cell service frequencies: jammed.

Wi-Fi: blocked.

Wireless comm unit frequency for the mercenary team to communicate: clear.

I watched the data report and repeated the three confirmations in my mind with each second that passed.

Jammed.

Blocked.

Clear.

Jammed.

Blocked.

Clear.

Jammed.

Blocked.

What the fuck?

Another device was interfering with the frequency of the comm units. It only took a few heartbeats for me to lock in on the rogue device's GPS signal.

Well, shit. I'd pinpointed my exact location. And the

signal wasn't coming from any of my equipment. Which meant it was one of Davis' devices. One he hadn't disclosed to me before the op.

Fucking satellite phone.

A few more heartbeats, and I decrypted the phone.

Davis had just sent a text. The message popped up on my screen: *I've been hired to kidnap your fiancée, Valentina Sanchez. Will return her to you for $50 mil. You have 6 minutes to decide.*

My stomach dropped.

A reply text came through almost instantaneously: *How do I know this is real?*

Davis: *Try to contact the men you assigned to guard her. My team has handled them. I want $50 mil. 5 minutes.*

Holy shit, Davis was betraying us to Adrián Rodríguez. I had to warn Andrés. Davis was armed with real firepower, and he could kill us all in a matter of seconds.

Damn it, I shouldn't have paid mercenaries to do this job. Obviously, Davis' services were for sale to the highest bidder. I'd thought this team was our best option, since I couldn't exactly ask my friends at the FBI to help us out.

Rodríguez texted back: *Deal. $50 mil. Where are you?*

Davis: *Not a chance. I'll deliver her to you. After you give me the down payment.*

Davis included instructions to wire half the funds to an offshore account. Rodríguez replied with an address where Davis was to bring Valentina.

I glanced at the clock on my laptop. Only four minutes until Andrés returned with his sister. I had to tell him what was going on, but I couldn't stop jamming cell reception or Davis might get tipped off.

Fuck. If Davis realized what I was doing, he would probably shoot me on the spot. I pressed a hand to my belly, thinking about my child.

But I couldn't let Andrés walk into an ambush. I'd be dead as soon as he returned to the SUV, anyway. Davis would kill both of us and take Valentina back to Rodríguez.

I had to chance it. Moving as surreptitiously as possible, I picked up my phone from where I'd left it resting on the seat beside me. I didn't have to look at the screen as I typed out my message; my thumb slid across the electronic keyboard with practiced ease.

Don't bring Valentina to SUV. Davis is dirty.

Using my free hand to operate my laptop, I restored cell service in the area and pressed the *send* button on my phone. Five seconds later, I jammed the frequency again.

I didn't have a moment to take a small breath of relief before a soft buzz sounded from the front seat. My heart sank. In the brief window I'd restored cell service so I could get my message to Andrés, a waiting text had come through to Davis' phone.

He immediately spun to face me, shoving his gun in my face.

"Close the laptop and drop your phone," he ground out.

Shit. I complied immediately, even though I was tempted to delay a few seconds to try to send another message to Andrés. But I couldn't gamble with my safety, not when it wasn't only my life at stake. I was in a pretty bleak situation, but I'd do everything in my power to protect my baby.

My laptop snapped closed, and my phone dropped down onto the floorboard. I'd been disarmed more effectively than if Davis had forced me to hand over a semi-automatic rifle. I'd just surrendered my most valuable weapons.

"What did you do?" Davis demanded, his thin lips peeled back from his teeth in a furious snarl. His ice blue eyes held no compassion, and I knew he wouldn't hesitate to pull the trigger if I so much as breathed in a way he didn't like.

"You won't be taking Valentina anywhere," I informed him in as calm a tone as I could manage. "I sent a message to Andrés. He won't bring her to you. You should let me out of the car and drive away. If anything happens to me, Andrés will kill you, and it won't be quick."

Davis cursed and ran his free hand over his buzzed blond hair. "Nosy fucking bitch. Rodríguez will kill me if I don't deliver."

"I guess you'd better let me go and start running," I reasoned. "Take the SUV. Get as much of a head start as you can. If you let me go now, I swear Andrés won't come after you."

He jerked his head to the side in a sharp refusal. "I'm not taking a vehicle you can track so easily. I have my own car waiting." The taut lines of rage eased from his harsh features, smoothing into calm resolution. "You're coming with me," he announced.

"What? Why?"

Davis raised his gun slightly, aiming dead between my eyes. "Shut the fuck up and do as I say. Hand me that laptop."

I picked it up and passed it to him. He tossed it into the passenger seat without taking his icy gaze from my face.

"Don't move an inch. If you go for your phone, you're dead. I'm getting out of the car now. Then, I'm going to open your door, and you'll follow me to my sedan. Don't even think about running or screaming for help. This whole op is already fucked, so I don't care about leaving your body behind for the cops to find. Got it?"

"Yeah." I barely breathed the word.

I couldn't afford to linger if Davis was determined to take me with him. Now that I'd sent my warning message to Andrés, there was no guarantee that he wouldn't come tearing across campus to get back to me, even if he knew that might be a suicide mission. He wasn't armed, and no matter how strong my husband might be, a bullet to the head would put him down.

All I could do was comply with Davis' demands and hope that Andrés could regroup, get the necessary weapons, and come after me. For now, I needed both of us alive, and I needed him to get Valentina somewhere safe.

When Davis got out of the driver's seat and quickly opened my door, I didn't hesitate to follow his orders. The possibility of catching him by surprise and attempting to disarm him flitted across my mind. He'd been forced to holster his weapon at his side to conceal it as we moved to his waiting black sedan, which was parked three spaces up from our SUV.

I dismissed that plan before it could fully form. I might have trained as a field agent, but I'd never excelled at hand-to-hand combat, and I was over a year out of practice, anyway. Even more importantly, I couldn't risk getting injured and losing my baby.

I allowed Davis to grip my elbow and steer me where he wanted me to go. When I slid into the passenger seat of his car, he snapped the door shut and settled into his own seat in a matter of seconds.

"I don't understand why you're taking me with you." I made a final attempt at reasoning with him as he turned the key in the ignition.

He didn't glance at me as he put the car in drive and pulled out into traffic. "I'm not going to Rodríguez emptyhanded."

My heart fluttered in my chest. "I don't mean anything to him."

"You can tell him where Moreno is taking Valentina."

"I could, but I won't." My voice remained steady, but my fingers trembled. I fisted my hands in my lap.

Davis didn't so much as glance at me as he spoke. I recognized the cold focus of a man on a mission. "I know Moreno is more than your employer. You were eye fucking each other the whole drive from the airport to UCLA, and judging by the way he kissed you, he's not going to let you go so easily. You're leverage."

Acid coated my tongue, but I swallowed it down. "Andrés won't trade Valentina for me, if that's what you're thinking."

Davis shrugged. "If he doesn't want to do that, then I'm sure you'll tell Rodríguez where he can find his fiancée. I heard he really took his time carving up the last person who tried to take Valentina from him. You'll talk eventually."

A metallic tang washed through my mouth, and I realized I'd bitten the inside of my cheek. I took a deep breath and tried to calm my racing heart. I might lose a lot more blood today if Adrián Rodríguez proved to be as sadistic as his reputation proclaimed.

CHAPTER 4
ANDRÉS

I hadn't taken two steps to close the remaining distance between me and Samantha when my phone buzzed in my pocket.

My stomach dropped. My phone shouldn't be receiving any messages. Not until we got back to the SUV and Samantha restored cell service.

Had I lingered too long talking to Valentina and run out of time?

I grabbed the device from my pocket and unlocked it to check the notification.

A text from Samantha: *Don't bring Valentina to SUV. Davis is dirty.*

A snarl slipped between my bared teeth.

"Andrés? What's going on?"

Valentina gripped my arm, but I was barely aware of her presence at my side. The entire world blurred around me, my vision washing red.

I wrenched free from my sister's hold. "Stay right here," I barked at her, already sprinting toward the SUV.

My heart pounded against my ribcage, sending fury and fear coursing through my system. I had to get to Samantha. Valentina would be exposed, but the men who'd been guarding her had been neutralized, and Rodríguez was no longer a threat.

Now, Davis was the threat. I'd left my Samantha with a calculated killer, and he was armed with a lethal weapon.

I didn't have a weapon of my own, but that didn't register as a problem in my mind. My bare hands were violent enough to rip apart anyone who threatened my wife.

I could see the black SUV parked where we'd left it at the curb, but my feet couldn't move fast enough to reach it. The windows were tinted so dark that I couldn't see the inside of the vehicle.

Dread twisted my gut, and I sprinted impossibly faster to get to her. I launched myself at the back door on the passenger side, grabbing the handle and wrenching it open.

An inhuman sound tore from my chest, something between a snarl and an agonized howl. Samantha was gone. The car was empty.

No blood. I assessed the scene in the space of a heartbeat. *He didn't shoot her. She's not dead. She's not dead.*

Her phone was on the floor, her laptop abandoned

on the front seat. She wouldn't have left them behind if she hadn't been forced to leave them.

Davis had taken Samantha.

But why? For ransom?

Fucking mercenaries.

I hastily checked my phone to see if I'd received any sort of message from Davis that might give me a clue about where or why he'd taken her.

No signal. Samantha had managed to get a message to me to warn me about Davis, but cell service was still down. He'd taken her laptop from her, and she hadn't been able to stop jamming the frequency.

"Andrés, what's going on?" Valentina approached, despite my command for her to stay away.

I slammed my fist into the side of the SUV, impotent rage washing through my system. "He took Samantha." My words were so harsh that they were barely discernable, but Valentina seemed to understand.

She cursed under her breath. "I'll call Adrián. He can help us find her."

I rounded on my sister. "How do you know Davis didn't take her on Rodríguez's orders?" I bellowed, unable to rein myself in.

Valentina paled. "If Adrián has anything to do with this, it's only because he thinks I'm in danger. I'll just call him and explain. Everything will be fine."

"Your fucking phone won't work. Fuck!"

"Okay," she replied, her voice hitching slightly despite her calm tone. "Let's get in the car and drive to my house. Adrián will help us. I promise. If he has anything to do with this, he won't hurt your wife. It's just a misunderstanding. And if Davis acted on his own, Adrián will be able to track him down."

Her reasonable plan calmed my roiling emotions for the space of a few heartbeats. Then, I registered that the keys were no longer in the ignition. Davis must have taken them with him. And I didn't know how to hotwire a car.

With every second that passed, Samantha was taken farther away from me. I felt the pull toward her like a tug on my soul.

"Let's get going," Valentina prompted, her words strained.

"I don't have the fucking keys."

"Shit." She drew in a sharp breath and grabbed my hand. "Come with me."

I remained rooted to the spot, barely registering that she was yanking on my arm. It felt wrong to move away from the place where I'd left Samantha, as though I'd be abandoning the only connection I had to her if I left the SUV.

"Come on," Valentina urged, pulling at me with all her strength. "I know someone who can help us. He's on campus. If we get to him, he'll be able to take us to Adrián."

I jerked my body away from the car and started moving. Valentina picked up the pace, running faster than I would have expected. I could surpass her with my longer strides, but I needed her to guide me. As it was, I was grateful for her speed.

We were probably attracting notice, sprinting across campus. I no longer cared about that. If Rodríguez truly wasn't my enemy, then it wouldn't matter if anyone saw my disfigurement and rumors of a monster with Valentina got back to him.

We arrived at the lecture hall where I'd first spotted Valentina, and she led me across the threshold. Our pace slowed as we moved through the building, but she strode with brisk purpose toward our destination.

We rounded a corner, and my focus instantly caught on the massive man who was leaning casually against the wall. He was a big fucker, jacked muscles straining against his black t-shirt. As soon as his dark eyes landed on my scarred face, he pushed away from the wall and assumed an aggressive stance. Monsters tended to recognize one another on a primal level.

Valentina stepped in front of me, coming to an abrupt stop. My first instinct was to shove past her and put myself between her and danger.

"Andrés, wait," she ordered sharply. "Mateo," she addressed the big motherfucker. "This is my brother, Andrés. He's not a threat. We need your help."

Mateo's head cocked to the side, his square jaw working as he ground his teeth. His eyes narrowed on my face, assessing me.

"Stop it," Valentina insisted, cutting through the

mounting tension between us. "Mateo, we need a ride back to the house. I can't get in touch with Adrián."

The animosity left his gaze as his attention turned back on her. "What's wrong with your phone?"

"Cell service is down," she explained quickly. "You won't be able to call him, either. Please, Mateo. I'll explain in the car. We have to get going."

The man hesitated, his lips pressing together in indecision. "I don't want to leave Sofia."

I didn't know who the fuck Sofia was, and I didn't care. Before I lost my tenuous hold on my rage, Valentina spoke up.

"Sofia will be fine. Class just started, and you know she won't be out of her lecture for an hour and a half. You can drive us to the house and get back here in time."

"I don't know—"

"Come with us right now, or I'll tell Adrián you chose to stand outside Sofia's completely safe classroom while I begged you for help." The threat was clear in Valentina's scathing tone. Maybe Rodríguez really did love her, if he allowed her the power to threaten his men.

Mateo spat out a curse. "If anything happens to Sofia while I'm gone—"

"Nothing's going to happen to her. Do you think I'd take you away from her if I thought she was in danger? You might be guarding her, but let's not pretend you're her bodyguard. Now, get moving."

I had no idea what was going on between Mateo, Sofia, and Valentina, but I barely wasted any of what was left of my rational thought processes puzzling it out. The imperative to find Samantha pounded through my brain, the thunderous sound of my racing heartbeat echoing in my ears.

Mateo dropped his aggressive stance and closed the distance between us. Valentina took my hand again and started pulling me along.

"Hurry," she urged Mateo, breaking into a jog. "We have to get back to Adrián." She squeezed my hand as we picked up the pace. "Everything's going to be fine, big brother. No one's going to hurt Samantha."

The worry that roughened her tone betrayed her lie. If Rodríguez had Samantha, my little pet wasn't safe from harm.

CHAPTER 5
SAMANTHA

"There's still time to turn around and take me back to Andrés," I said, fighting to keep the tremor from my voice. Davis had driven us into a neighborhood that was obviously inhabited by the ultra-rich. Greenery surrounded the winding road, and homes were hidden down long driveways. There was some serious real estate tucked away behind those trees, and the privacy factor made my gut clench.

Once the wrought iron gates before us opened up, there wouldn't be any going back. I'd be locked away on Adrián Rodríguez's estate, isolated and alone.

Davis was on his phone, likely typing out another text to Rodríguez to tell him we'd arrived. When he finished sending his message, he glanced over at me.

"Not happening," he replied curtly. "As it is, I won't get the rest of my payout from Rodríguez. If I don't show at all, he'll hunt me down and kill me. He has far more resources at his disposal than Moreno. The fact that you hired me proves that you don't have any loyal people of your own. I'm going to deliver you to Rodríguez and get the hell out of town with twenty-five million in my account. It's half of what I wanted, but it's better than nothing."

The gates eased open, and Davis drove in.

Okay, I reasoned, struggling to remain calm. *I'll be okay. Andrés will figure out where I am, and he'll come get me. I just need to stay alive until he arrives.*

I realized I was pressing my palm against my belly, and I forced my hand back to my knee. I'd do whatever it took to protect my baby. I just had to trust in Andrés. And hope that Rodríguez wouldn't start carving me up immediately.

My stomach turned, and I swallowed back bile.

Davis drove for a couple minutes before the house came into view. The sprawling Spanish-style mansion probably had plenty of rooms to imprison me. Or torture me. Or...

I took a breath, cutting off my erratic thoughts before my wits became scrambled by fear. There was no way I'd be able to fight my way out of this, but violence had never been my strong suit. I needed my mind clear if I was going to survive long enough for Andrés to get here.

If he makes it here alive. I couldn't stop that particular unbidden thought when Rodríguez stepped out onto the porch, flanked by two burly men. I recognized him from the research I'd done on Valentina's captors. He had a cruel sort of beauty about him, with his sculpted face and tailored suit. Even from this distance, I could discern his glittering, pale green eyes. I recognized a predator when I saw one, no matter how alluring he might appear.

All three men were armed. The guards trained their weapons on Davis, marking him through the windshield. Rodríguez held his piece casually at his side, as though it were an extension of his arm.

Davis put the sedan in park and held up his hands in a show of goodwill. Rodríguez gave him silent permission to get out of the car with a single nod.

"Stay put," Davis ordered as he opened the door and stood to face Rodríguez.

"Tell your partner to get out, too," Rodríguez commanded, tipping his head in my direction without taking his eyes off Davis' face.

Davis kept his hands up as he spoke. "She's not my partner. She's working with the man who took your fiancée."

Rodríguez's brows drew together, shadowing his remarkable eyes. "Where is Valentina?" he demanded on a snarl.

Davis gestured at me. "Ask her. The bitch intercepted our messages and warned him not to bring Valentina to me. I brought her here so you could—"

Rodríguez raised his weapon and fired three rounds

directly into Davis' chest without another word. The man was dead before he hit the ground.

Then, glowing green eyes focused on me.

Oh, fuck.

He prowled to the car and opened my door. His weapon was back at his side rather than aimed at me, but I knew that didn't mean shit. He'd just proven how quickly he could end someone's life without batting an eye.

"Where is Valentina?" he growled, his predator's eyes burning into me from above.

I lifted my chin and met his intense stare. "I don't know."

That was true enough. I had no idea where Andrés might take his sister to ensure her safety while he gathered the resources he'd need to come after me. It was possible he'd take her to the airport and put her on the jet back to our island, but I didn't know that for sure.

Rodríguez raised his weapon again, moving with smooth grace as he pressed the barrel of the gun to my forehead. "You have three seconds to tell me where she is."

"You can't kill me. If you kill me, you won't have any way to find her. You won't have any leads or leverage. So, that's a really bad idea. You definitely shouldn't do that."

I swallowed the stream of anxious words that threatened to spill from my lips. Babbling wouldn't help my case.

Rodríguez's nostrils flared, his crystalline eyes glittering with rage. "Get out of the car."

He withdrew his gun, allowing me space to unbuckle my seatbelt and clumsily get to my feet. I wasn't graceful at the best of times, and fear made my knees weak.

Rodríguez's iron fingers closed around my upper arm. He didn't squeeze hard enough to bruise, but he could shatter my bones with very little effort.

"Don't disturb me for any reason," he ordered his guards. His voice was icy, his cold control far more terrifying than if he'd been shouting threats at me.

He started walking, pulling me along beside him. I stumbled but managed to remain upright. I had a feeling he would have continued dragging me where he wanted to take me, even if I'd fallen. He probably wouldn't care if I dislocated my shoulder.

He wasn't taking me into the house. Instead, he directed us over a spacious back patio that provided a stunning view of the city. We didn't pause to take in the vista. He led me onto a gently sloping, lush green lawn, which was sheltered by trees. There wasn't a neighboring home in sight. Or earshot, most likely. I could scream myself hoarse, and no one would hear me.

My skin pebbled, a block of ice forming in the pit of my stomach. We were walking toward a shed. Nothing good happened in a place like that. I'd been concerned about being imprisoned in his fancy mansion, but this basic structure was designed to get messy. Rodríguez wouldn't worry about bloodstains on the concrete floor.

Fuck, fuck, fuck...

My feet stalled, my body instinctively recoiling. He didn't seem to notice my small act of resistance; he kept walking with brisk purpose, and I had no choice but to follow.

By the time we reached the shed, my heart had pounded up into my throat, threatening to choke off my air supply. Rodríguez hadn't so much as looked at me as he'd dragged me across his property, and he didn't spare me a glance as he turned the knob and pushed open the shed's metal door. His silence and cold disregard for me as a human being were terrifying enough, but then I noticed his jaw tick as he ground his teeth. I recognized rage in the taut lines of his defined features. He appeared aloof and collected, but Rodríguez was a man on the edge of control. If he snapped, he'd kill me instantly and brutally. The prospect of interrogation made nausea roll through my stomach, but I couldn't save my baby if I didn't survive long enough for Andrés to rescue me.

A single metal chair waited in the center of the cramped space. It gleamed dully under the spare light-bulb overhead. The unyielding metal was spotless, but I knew it had likely been painted red with gore many times. It would be easy to hose down after...

I drew in a shaky breath, struggling to keep my mind clear.

Rodríguez shoved me down into the chair and grabbed a small coil of rope from a table set beside it. I kept my eyes trained forward as he wrenched my arms behind my back and secured them with a tight knot. I didn't want to look at what else lay on that table. As it was, my wild imagination was almost as horrifying as facing the torture implements.

He stood back, towering over me. My gaze was drawn to his, and I found myself locked beneath his glowing green glare.

"Who are you working for?" His controlled tone held a steely edge.

My fingers shook, and I jerked against the rope that bound me to the chair. "I'm not working for anyone," I insisted tremulously.

If I stuck to the truth, maybe I could buy myself some time. Outright lies would lead to harsher methods of extracting answers.

Rodríguez leaned into me, bracing his big hands on the arms of the chair. His cruel, beautiful face filled my vision. He was close enough that I could smell his expensive cologne. Perfect white teeth flashed as he growled at me.

"I don't usually hurt women, but I will tear you apart piece by piece until you tell me where I can find your employer. If he doesn't surrender her to me, I'll tear him apart, too. Valentina is mine, and I will get her back, no matter what it takes."

Defiance surged through my terror. I wouldn't

betray Andrés, even if it did cost my life. "I'm not telling you shit. You'll never see Valentina again."

His muscles rippled and flexed, and he bared his teeth like a wild animal. The man was insane with possessive rage.

Suddenly, he gripped my jaw, forcing me to face the objects on the table beside me. The wicked instruments for my torture glinted under the dim light. For a moment, I saw Cristian smirking down at me, scraping his hunting knife across my skin. My stomach rolled, my entire body convulsing in horror.

"No one will keep Valentina from me," Rodríguez snarled. "You will tell me where I can find her. How quickly the pain ends is up to you."

"Please," I whispered, the truth slipping from me before I could think. "I'm pregnant."

Rodríguez recoiled from me, a frustrated roar echoing through the shed. He retreated a few steps, until his back hit the door. He braced his hands on the metal behind him, as though anchoring himself there.

"Tell me where I can find her." His pale eyes were wild, his words rough with something like panic. The man staring at me with a mix of horror and desperation was closer to the brink of madness than the cruel killer who'd tied me to this chair.

Confusion threaded through my terror. This wasn't the reaction of a sadistic captor who wanted his possession returned to him.

I wasn't the only one in this shed who was afraid.

My mind raced, reevaluating the situation in light of this new information. Valentina was marrying Rodríguez tomorrow. She's been allowed to enroll in college and given the freedom to move around the city, even if she had been guarded at all times. She'd been the one to put in the order with the florist. She'd chosen the flowers for her wedding.

Because she wanted to marry Adrián Rodríguez.

"You love her." The words popped out of my mouth.

His entire body jerked, dark shadows pooling over his eyes beneath his drawn brows. He pressed his lips together, as though holding back the admission. He didn't want me to know that he loved her, because he thought his vulnerability would give me power over him.

I took a breath, trying to sort through the best way to reason with him. "Listen, Adrián. There's been a mistake. We didn't know—"

A deafening *bang* shattered the tension between us like a bullet through glass, and I shrieked in shock. Bright sunlight seared my vision, momentarily blinding me after the dimness of the shed. I registered rough, animal sounds, and for a moment, I thought a rabid dog had burst into the shed.

I blinked the sunlight from my eyes. The dull thud of flesh hitting flesh accompanied the scene that coalesced around me.

Andrés was on top of Adrián, pinning his body against the concrete floor as he brought his fist down on my captor's jaw. My husband's face twisted with feral rage, his scar drawn deep into his cheek. I'd only seen him wear this terrifying, furious mask once before: when Cristian had threatened my life.

He'd killed his brother that night. He'd kill Adrián if I didn't stop him.

"Andrés!" I screamed his name to call him back to me before he did something he might regret.

His big body jerked, as though I'd slammed the full force of my weight into him. My desperate cry caught his attention, distracting him from his murderous intent.

Adrián took advantage of his moment of hesitation, using the opening to get the upper hand. He shoved Andrés away, grabbing his shirt and wrenching him upright. Adrián slammed my husband back against the wall, and his head cracked against the heavy metal beam behind him.

"Stop! Adrián, stop!" Valentina appeared in the ruined doorway, her delicate features twisted in horror.

Just as my scream had distracted Andrés, Valentina's distress seemed to pierce Adrián's body like a knife.

Andrés' lips peeled back from his teeth, and I knew he was about to punch Adrián again.

"Andrés, don't!" I twisted against the rope that kept me trapped. I had to get to him and end this before someone died. Because it was clear that neither of them would stop until the other was eliminated.

"He's my brother," Valentina yelled, darting toward

the enraged men. She grabbed Adrián's arm, as though she could physically restrain him. "Adrián, please. Just stop and listen to me. I'm right here. Andrés brought me back to you."

"Andrés, look at me," I demanded as soon as Valentina reached her fiancé. My husband's black eyes fixed on me immediately. His body swelled with rage at the sight of me bound, so I quickly continued reasoning with him. "I'm okay," I promised. "I'm not hurt. This is a misunderstanding. Valentina wants to be with Adrián. He loves her. He won't hurt her, and he didn't hurt me."

Valentina tried to reason with the man she loved, too. "My brother wanted to save me. He didn't know I'm with you willingly. This is his wife, Samantha. He's worried for her safety. What would you do to someone who threatened me?"

Adrián abruptly shoved away from Andrés, placing his body in front of Valentina.

"Andrés." I kept his attention on me to prevent him from attacking Adrián again. "Can you help me up? I'm not hurt, but I need your help, okay?"

His nostrils flared, his dark eyes sharp on my face. He pushed away from the wall and closed the distance between us, not sparing his enemy another glance. His entire focus was centered on me.

"Everything's okay," I swore, soothing the beast that lived inside the man I loved. "I just need you to untie me. Adrián didn't do anything. He didn't hurt me," I reiterated. If Andrés thought I'd been harmed in any way, he would turn on Valentina's fiancé again, no matter what I said.

He dropped to one knee before me, his big hand cupping my cheek. He turned my face gently, studying me for any sign of injury. I met his keen gaze with a steady stare, taking deep, calming breaths. After a few heartbeats, he mirrored me, and the violent tension eased from his massive frame.

His arms closed around me, his fingers finding the knot at my wrists and freeing me with expert ease. As soon as he untied me, he pulled me into a fierce embrace.

"Samantha," he rasped my name, his body shuddering with relief as he breathed in my scent.

"I'm right here," I promised, tucking my face closer against his chest. "I'm safe."

I heard Valentina murmuring to Adrián in a similar low, reassuring tone. After a few minutes, their footsteps sounded on the concrete. Andrés didn't release me or glance in their direction.

I couldn't see anything other than his massive chest, but Valentina's request reached me as they moved away.

"Just wait outside the house, big brother. I'm going to talk to Adrián, and we can all meet each other properly when everyone's cooled off."

Andrés didn't respond, and I wasn't certain if he was really capable of comprehending his sister's words.

I pressed my palm over his heart, tethering him to me. "Hey," I said gently. "Can you take me out of here?

There's a nice patio behind the house. Let's go wait there."

His grip shifted on my body, and he lifted me with ease. I was happy for him to carry me away from the shed. I'd put on a brave front for him, but I'd been really fucking scared just a few minutes ago.

The warm sunlight hit my skin as we stepped out onto the lawn. I drew in a shaky breath and turned my face into my husband's chest, seeking his strength. I marveled that we were okay. I'd thought our lives were on the line.

We were all safe now: Andrés, me, and our baby.

CHAPTER 6
ANDRÉS

It took concerted effort to restrain myself from crushing Samantha's slight body as I held her close to my chest. I matched her deep, calming breaths, easing most of the violent tension from my muscles. My instincts told me to hold her with all my strength, as though she was my prized possession that Rodríguez might try to take away from me again.

I pressed my face closer to hers, nuzzling her silky hair so I could feel her softness against my scarred cheek. Her slender fingers closed around my nape, locking me in place. My little pet was just as desperate for my nearness as I was for hers.

A low stream of words in my native tongue dropped from my lips, the reassuring cadence meant to ground me as well as comfort her.

Lo siento.

I hadn't realized I'd said the apology aloud until she

pulled back from me, capturing my face in her delicate hand.

"Hey," she said softly, piercing my soul with her aquamarine gaze. "There's nothing to be sorry for."

"He took you," I growled, my arms tightening around her before I could hold back the impulse.

She didn't seem to mind my harsh hold; she remained relaxed and supple in my iron grip.

"*Davis* took me," she countered firmly, "Adrián didn't hurt me. He didn't want to. He was just trying to frighten me into telling him where he could find Valentina. He really loves her, Andrés. He was scared for her safety when he thought she'd been taken. Just like you were scared for me."

"Where is Davis now?" I demanded. If I couldn't punish Rodríguez for taking my Samantha from me, then I'd rip apart the mercenary instead.

"He's dead." She trailed her fingertips over my cheek, soothing me. "Adrián killed him as soon as we got here."

I pulled her closer to my chest. "I don't want my little sister with that drug lord," I ground out. "He's dangerous."

She fixed me with a steady stare. "And what would you have done to Davis if you'd gotten to him first?"

I gnashed my teeth. My pet was too clever some-times. It would be much easier to settle into my rage than look at the situation objectively.

"Andrés?" she prompted, refusing to allow me to evade the question.

A series of bloody images flashed across my mind as I envisioned all the ways I would have mutilated Davis before finally letting him die.

"You don't want to know," I admitted. I'd promised my wife I wouldn't kill anyone while we went in to rescue Valentina, and she wouldn't approve of the vicious things I would have done to the mercenary if I'd gotten my hands on him.

"That's what I thought," Samantha said smoothly. "I can't say that Adrián Rodríguez is a good man. He's a ruthless criminal, but he loves your sister. She wants to marry him, doesn't she?"

My scar drew tight on a frown. "She says she does. But how can she know what she wants? She's been imprisoned by the Rodríguez family since she was fourteen. It would be better for her to marry someone else."

"But she doesn't love someone else," Samantha reasoned. "She loves Adrián."

I jerked my head sharply to the side. "That's probably because she doesn't know how to love anyone else. She was trapped with that family for years. She didn't have a choice."

Samantha's copper brows rose, and she fixed me with a challenging stare. "And what do you think my friends at the FBI say about my relationship with you? They don't approve. They don't think I have a choice. But I do, and I

59

choose you. It doesn't matter what circumstances brought us together. I love you, Andrés. I always will. No one would be able to take me from you and convince me otherwise."

I blew out a long sigh, defeated. "I love you, too. I wouldn't let anyone take you from me." I'd almost lost my mind just a few hours ago when Davis had tried to steal her. I would have done anything necessary to get her back.

A pinging sound distracted me momentarily, but I realized it was just Mateo's phone receiving a text. The massive man had been keeping an eye on us while we sat on the patio. He hadn't threatened me in any way, and he kept a careful, respectful distance. But he'd been watching me, nonetheless.

I supposed I would have done the same, in Rodríguez's position. I wouldn't have allowed a man who'd just attacked me to lounge outside my home without a guard.

"Adrián says you can come inside," Mateo announced. "He wants to talk to you."

I pushed up off the cushioned chair I'd been sitting on for the last hour while I'd kept Samantha in my arms.

"You can put me down now," she urged.

I glowered at her, my first instinct telling me to keep her tucked as close to me as possible.

She stared right back at me, implacably calm and reasonable. "We're safe here. Valentina wants you to meet her fiancé. You don't have to carry me around like a caveman. That would be weird. Okay?"

I didn't care about adhering to social norms. I just cared about Samantha's safety.

"The boss says you're welcome guests here," Mateo interjected. "No one's going to hurt your wife. Valentina won't allow it."

I would have been skeptical of his assertion, but the declaration that Valentina wouldn't allow it swayed me. I realized that she truly did wield power in this house. Possibly more than Rodríguez himself. If such a notoriously ruthless man allowed my sister to influence his decisions, he really must love her.

I carefully set Samantha down on her feet, my touch lingering around her waist. She firmly caught my hand in hers and started walking across the patio, urging me to accompany her. My fierce pet was too brave for her own good sometimes, but I allowed her to march toward the man who'd been holding her hostage and terrorizing her only an hour ago.

The memory of her tied to the chair in that shed made my muscles tense with rage, and she squeezed my hand in silent comfort, reassuring me.

I took a breath. I should be the one reassuring *her*.

As always, Samantha's strength and goodness reminded me that I needed to be better if I ever had a hope of deserving her. I would face Adrián Rodríguez, and I wouldn't try to kill him this time. If Samantha could forgive him so easily, I'd try to emulate her.

Mateo walked ahead of us, ushering us around the massive mansion until we reached the front door.

Valentina waited at the threshold, the soft lines of her heart-shaped face drawn sharp with anxiety. As soon as she caught sight of me, she shifted to close the distance that separated us. Rodríguez placed a restraining hand on her hip, pulling her back against his body and tucking her close to his side. His strange, luminous green eyes fixed on me, glinting with warning.

Without thinking, I mirrored his movement, tugging Samantha closer to me so I could wrap my arm around her and shield her fragile body. I heard her huff out an exasperated breath, but she knew better than to try to pull away. My control over my roiling emotions was tenuous, at best, and if she tried to extricate herself from my protective hold, that control would snap. I needed to feel her safe beside me.

We came to a stop at the edge of the front porch, several feet separating Samantha from Rodríguez. I wanted to go to Valentina, but I wouldn't put my wife at risk.

"Can I go now, boss?" Mateo asked. I'd only been peripherally aware of the hulking man as a secondary potential threat. He might be huge, but he was silent as a shadow.

Rodríguez's jaw ticked, but he didn't take his eyes off me or give his guard permission to leave.

"Adrián," Valentina said, all softness and persuasion. "Mateo wants to get back to Sofia. I promised him he could. She should be out of class by now. She really shouldn't be left alone. I already told you that Andrés won't try to take me away from you. He came to find me. Everything else has been a misunderstanding." She turned a pointed stare on me. "Isn't that right, big brother?"

"Of course it is," Samantha said immediately. "I misread the situation. The extraction plan was my idea. So really, this is on me. Sorry if I—"

She stopped her apology on a little gasp when my fingers curved into her hip, squeezing hard in rebuke. She was trying to put herself in Rodríguez's crosshairs and take the heat off me.

Not fucking happening. My pet was in so much trouble when I got her somewhere private. She should know better.

Rodríguez's glowing stare shifted to her. "You're the one who found Valentina?"

"Samantha was looking for my sister as a favor to me," I snapped. "She's not responsible for anything that happened today."

She stiffened in my hold. "Andrés," she hissed my name indignantly. "I've been trying to help you find Valentina for over a year. I came up with the plan. I covered our tracks and had your backs. Don't you dare say I had nothing to do with reuniting you with your sister. This whole op was my idea."

"Thank you," Rodríguez said before I could throw my wife over my shoulder and haul her away for punishment.

I blinked and focused on him, but his full attention

was fixed on Samantha. His pale eyes were intense but strangely earnest. "Valentina has missed her brother. I wasn't able to find Andrés for her. I'm glad you brought them together. I'm sorry if I scared you earlier."

Samantha waved away his apology, as though his attempted torture was of no consequence. "That's okay. Andrés would have done the same thing in your situation, I'm sure. We're all good now. I know you wouldn't have hurt me anyway, would you?"

He cut his gaze away, as though he was ashamed of his weakness. "No," he muttered. "I wouldn't have."

Mateo cleared his throat pointedly, interrupting the emotional moment.

"Oh, just go on, Mateo," Valentina sighed. "We're fine."

Rodríguez spared a brief nod to his man, dismissing him. Valentina really did call the shots around here. The small display of the true power dynamic in this house helped ease the last of my fury with Rodríguez. I believed his admission that he wouldn't have actually hurt Samantha.

"I'm so glad you're here, big brother," Valentina said, her dark eyes shining. "I've missed you so much." Her voice hitched, but she continued on. "I'm marrying Adrián tomorrow. I know today has been...tense. But I want you to be with us at the wedding. More than anything. Will you stay?"

I hesitated. Lingering in America hadn't been part of the plan. If Samantha's friends at the FBI caught wind of the fact that I was in the States, they'd come after me. They'd try to take my wife away.

She placed her hand on my forearm, silently lending her support and approval. "It's okay," she said softly. "No one knows we're in LA. We're safe here."

"Yes, you are," Rodríguez swore. "My people will protect you."

"Adrián..." Valentina said her fiancé's name in a cajoling tone, prompting him to say something more. He stared down at her. She stared right back, a challenge in the strong lines of her smaller frame.

He pressed a tender kiss to her forehead. The sweet show of affection from the sadistic drug lord was completely at odds with his reputation for abject cruelty.

His attention turned back on me, all animosity gone from his pale eyes. "I'm sorry I scared your wife. You are both more than welcome at our wedding. I would be honored if you'd give us your blessing. Valentina would like you to walk her down the aisle."

A refusal teased at the tip of my tongue. I didn't want to give my little sister away to a criminal.

"Please, Andrés," Valentina beseeched my approval. "You're my family, but Adrián's my family, too. I've always loved him, ever since we were kids. I want to marry him, and I want you to be there with me."

"It's true," Adrián interjected. "I've loved Valentina since I was sixteen years old. I let her go once, but never again. I'll never allow anyone separate us or cause her pain."

"See?" Samantha urged quietly. "It's okay, Andrés. This is a good thing. They're happy together. Just like we are."

The reminder that my relationship with Samantha seemed unconventional to outside observers helped sway me. I might be a monster, but I would lay down my life a thousand times over to protect Samantha. If Rodríguez would do the same for my sister, then I could overlook his criminal lifestyle.

"Yes," I agreed, my throat tight. "I'll walk you down the aisle, Valentina."

She beamed at me, and I caught a flash of the carefree girl she'd once been right before she launched herself at me. Samantha stepped away, giving me space to embrace my sister. Her small body shuddered, and I realized I was shaking, too.

"I didn't think I'd ever see you again. I was so worried that you were dead." Her warm tears wet my shirt.

A matching heat trailed down my cheeks, as well, but I didn't feel any shame at the display of raw emotion. After more than fifteen years of separation, my family was finally whole again. I had my sister back, and my wife stood at my side. I'd never felt so complete. Before I'd met Samantha, I'd spent years in isolation, growing cold and cruel. Now, I was with the only two people who had ever mattered to me. The gratitude and relief that surged through me was almost overwhelming.

Valentina pulled away slightly, so she could look up at me. I hungrily drank in her features, memorizing the more mature shape of her face. We'd been robbed of our childhood together, but I'd never stopped being her big brother. I never would.

Her dark eyes landed on my scarred cheek, reminding me that my face had changed far more than hers.

"What happened to you?" she asked softly.

"Cristian," I bit out his loathsome name. Samantha had helped me let go of the humiliation that haunted me over the memory of my torture at my brother's hands, but now, guilt swelled. "I'm sorry I didn't protect you from him. He sold you, and I didn't do anything to stop him. I let him—"

Valentina shushed me, placing her hand over the furrow in my cheek, as though she could heal the mark with her gentle touch. "You did everything you could," she reassured me. "That's all in the past now. He can't hurt us anymore. Adrián says Cristian is dead. Isn't that right?"

"Yes," I confirmed with savage satisfaction. "I killed him."

"I'm glad," Valentina replied with savagery of her own. Neither of us would shed a tear over the loss of our older brother. I should have done the job years earlier. Fear had held me back, but I didn't have to be afraid anymore. Samantha had liberated me from that life of cowardice and shame.

"I can't believe you're really here," Valentina said thickly. "Everything is perfect now. Will you stay? After the wedding, I mean."

I hesitated. I didn't want to leave my sister so soon, but it would be unwise to stay Stateside for longer than necessary. Samantha's little blackout that she'd coordinated around UCLA this afternoon wouldn't have gone unnoticed, especially considering that she hadn't been able to undo her work before Davis had taken her. By now, law enforcement had likely located our getaway vehicle and her abandoned laptop.

"We have some time," Samantha supplied, as though reading my thoughts. "I scrubbed my biometric data from the FBI database, so if anyone pulls prints off that laptop, I won't pop up in the system. I can always run interference on security cams around the wedding venue tomorrow. We won't get flagged by any facial recognition systems. I can't hold off my friends at the Bureau forever, but they did lose their best asset when I left, so I can definitely buy us more time."

"You're an FBI agent?" Valentina asked, her attention turning on Samantha.

"Well, sort of. I used to be. I'm kind of a rogue agent now. Like, I still fight crime and whatnot, it's just on my own terms. You don't have to worry about me ratting you out to my friends at the Bureau. This is none of their business. I mean, if I were still an agent and had never met Andrés, I'd totally be investigating the shit out of Adrián. But I won't," she added quickly. "I did a ton of research, and I'm not a huge fan of the drug trafficking or, you know, the murdering people stuff, but you seem to stick to your own turf wars. You don't kill innocent people, and you're not involved in human trafficking. So, I'll let it slide. There are worse bad guys in the world who could use a good ass-kicking. I'll focus on them, instead."

"That's very generous of you," Rodríguez said drily.

"No problem," Samantha replied, as though it was no big deal and she was doing him a favor. "We're family now, and I won't turn on my family. Just try not to do anything too shady, or my friends will totally come after you. I'd rather not get into that situation, so be cool, okay?"

Rodríguez chuckled, and I breathed a small sigh of relief. Samantha could have gotten herself into trouble with all her warnings, but he seemed to find her rambling charming.

"I'll try," he allowed.

"Thank you, Samantha," Valentina said with genuine gratitude. "Anything you need to make sure you can both safely attend the wedding, just let me know. You can fix the security footage around the venue?"

"Oh yeah." Samantha waved her hand as though it was already taken care of. "Super simple. I'll just need a laptop for five minutes at some point before the ceremony tomorrow. Andrés and I can go back home after the reception. Buy you'll have to come visit us. We have this awesome island and a guest room in our house that we've never had a reason to use. I mean, we're the only people who live on the island, so I don't even know why we have a guest room. Well, I guess this is why. Now, you can come stay with us whenever."

Valentina grinned. "I'll come as soon as I can. The next break from classes, for sure. We could go on vacation. Right, Adrián?"

"Whatever you want, *conejita.*"

Rodríguez's bemused expression matched my own feelings. Somehow, I'd gone from wanting to kill him this morning to accepting him as my brother-in-law. While the women we loved made vacation plans.

I shrugged. If Rodríguez could get over this afternoon's unpleasant events and get on board with playing family, I could, too.

CHAPTER 7
ANDRÉS

"**Y**ou can stay here, big brother," Valentina said, gesturing for me to take Samantha into one of the guest rooms in her sprawling home. "I'll send someone out to get fresh clothes for both of you. Will you join us for dinner tonight?"

"Aren't you hosting a rehearsal dinner?" Samantha interjected, pausing at my side.

Valentina's glossy black hair swayed around her face as she shook her head. "I'm canceling it. I'd rather have dinner with my family. Adrián and I don't need to rehearse our wedding. It's not my first time getting married, and I'm sure he can figure out what to do."

A shadow passed over her eyes at the mention of her first marriage, but her flippant tone indicated that she'd prefer to joke about the situation than dwell on her true feelings. I wanted to know what had happened to my little sister, but I didn't feel like pressing for details, either. Valentina might have been in love with Adrián Rodríguez since she was a teenager, but she'd been forced to marry another man. I was all too familiar with the ugliest parts of our criminal underworld, and I could easily guess what had happened to Valentina.

For the first time, I registered gratitude that she was with Adrián. He claimed he'd always loved her and that he would protect her. Whatever she'd been through in the past, it was clear now that Adrián would slaughter anyone who tried to harm her. I might not like that she was marrying a drug lord, but there were advantages to the absolute devotion of a sadistic madman. No one would ever hurt my sister again.

"So, you'll come to dinner?" Valentina prompted. "Our chef can put something together in a couple hours. It'll just be the four of us in the dining room, so we don't need to worry about leaving the grounds. I know Samantha can cover your tracks, but I'd rather not go out in public more than absolutely necessary."

"Good call," Samantha approved. "We'd love to have dinner with you and Adrián. Wouldn't we, Andrés?" She poked her elbow into my side, urging me to agree.

"Yes," I replied. "But if you wouldn't mind, I need to talk to my wife about everything that's happened today. Privately."

Samantha instantly caught the low threat in my tone. She'd let her mouth run away with her when she'd spoken to Rodríguez. Just because everything had worked out peacefully didn't mean she wasn't going to be punished for putting herself at risk. I needed to feel her flesh heat beneath my harsh hands, needed to brand every inch of her body with my touch. After almost losing her today, my gut burned with the impulse to dominate her until she softened and submitted. I needed to hear her call me *Master* and promise that she belonged to me, now and forever.

"Um, that's okay," Samantha said, her voice higher than usual. "We should all keep hanging out before dinner. I mean, I don't need to change clothes or anything, if we're just eating at the house."

She tried to edge away from me. I wrapped my hand around her nape and anchored her in place at my side.

Valentina glanced from my face to Samantha's pink cheeks. "I think I'll give you two some privacy," she said after a moment. She fixed me with one final, significant stare. "I know you're a good man, Andrés. I'm sure you just want to spend some time with your wife after worrying about her this afternoon. You should make sure she's okay."

"I'm fine," Samantha insisted.

Valentina offered her a sympathetic smile. "You're definitely safe in our home. I'll see you both at dinner."

As soon as my sister retreated down the long hallway, my full focus centered on Samantha. Keeping my hold on her neck, I firmly guided her into the bedroom and shut the door behind us. The room was spacious and luxurious in an understated way; shades of tan and cream emphasized the enormity of Rodríguez's home, and a huge sliding glass door revealed the lush green grounds behind the house, which rolled out to a distant view of the city.

I only spared the space a cursory glance to ensure we were completely alone. No one was guarding us. And we were far enough away from the common spaces of the house that I was fairly confident no one would hear my naughty pet cry out and beg for mercy. I doubted anyone in Rodríguez's employ would interfere, anyway.

Samantha tried to edge away from me again, her slight body radiating nervous tension as she sought to put distance between us.

A warning growl slipped through my teeth, and I jerked her against me, hooking my free arm around her lower back to trap her in place. Her chest pressed tight to mine, and I could feel the rise and fall of her panting breaths, the rapid beat of her heart. Her nearness calmed my heart to its normal rhythm for the first time since I'd realized Davis had taken her.

Her shining eyes were wide, her pupils dilated. She licked her lush lips, a nervous tic she displayed when she was both anxious and aroused.

"Listen, Andrés. I—"

My fingers sank into her hair, tangling the copper strands around my fist as I forced her head back. Her pulse jumped at her throat.

"Quiet, *cosita*." My roiling emotions finally began to calm as I settled into my control over her. "I don't have one of your pretty gags, but I will find something to tame your tongue if necessary. No more arguing or talking out of turn. You put yourself at risk today. You shouldn't have spoken to Rodríguez like that."

"But I just explained what was going on," she protested, the defensive words popping out before she could hold herself back. "I talked us out of trouble, not into it. Davis would have killed both of us hours ago if I hadn't bought us time. I tried to convince him not to take me with him, but he did, and I couldn't stop that. He would have shot me on the spot if I'd challenged him. So, I let him take me to Adrián. And everything worked out, right? We're—"

I pulled sharply on her hair, and she stopped babbling on a gasp.

"Tell me exactly what Rodríguez did," I commanded.

"That doesn't matter now. Really, I—"

"Do not test me," I warned. "You have a punishment coming already. Answer my questions, or the consequences will only get worse."

She trembled against me, and more of my lingering tension eased. I'd stopped fighting my twisted nature a long time ago. Samantha responded to my darker needs; she accepted all of me. She even loved the monster in me, even though she feared it.

I drank in her fear like a man dying of thirst. If she was shaking in my harsh hold, she was real and safe. My pet had returned to the cage of my arms, and she wasn't going anywhere.

"Adrián was just asking me questions," she said on a tremulous whisper. "He just wanted to know where Valentina was so he could get her back. He thought you were my employer, and he wanted to know how to find you. But I didn't tell him anything," she added quickly.

My gut tightened, a shadow of my anger returning. "He would have tortured you for answers eventually," I ground out. "You should have told him where to find me. I would have handled him."

Her eyes flashed, defiance slicing through her fear. "I would never betray you."

I crushed her body closer to mine. "You should have trusted me to keep you safe. You should have told him everything he wanted to know, so he would leave you alone and come after me."

Her delicate jaw set in a hard line. "I did trust you. I trusted that you'd figure out where I was and come for me. But I wasn't going to give Adrián information that would allow him to ambush you. Besides, none of this matters now. Everything worked out fine."

"It matters to me," I growled. "Never do something like that again."

The anger cleared from her eyes, her features softening. "I won't, because I'll never be in a situation like that again. We're safe now. And we always will be, because we have each other's backs. We'll go home after the wedding tomorrow, and no one will be able to find us. No one will be able to hurt me. Or you. I won't let them."

I eased my harsh hold around her waist and trailed my fingers down her throat. Samantha's bravery awed me. I'd descended into madness when Davis took her from me. My clever pet might tend to ramble when she was nervous, but her formidable mind was a more powerful weapon than my brute strength.

I pressed a reverent kiss to her forehead, holding her in place with my grip on her hair. She blew out a shuddering sigh, her warm breath fanning my neck.

"*Te amo, mí sirenita*," I murmured, rubbing my scarred cheek against her soft, flawless skin.

Her slender fingers slid up into my hair, urging me closer. "I love you too," she promised.

I closed the hairsbreadth of distance between us and caressed her lips with mine. I kept my commanding grip on her hair, but I explored her mouth slowly, savoring her. I still intended to reprimand her, but there were other ways to reinforce the lesson than handling her body harshly. I wanted her to feel my control, my ownership of every inch of her flesh. I could do whatever I wanted to her, manipulate her pleasure and wield it as a tool for her punishment just as effectively as I could lash her with my whip.

My hands finally left her hair and throat, trailing down her sides to trace the curve of her hips. I fisted the material of her thin cotton t-shirt and eased it up her torso, stripping her at the pace I desired while I held her lips captive in mine.

Her hands were more frenzied as she tore at my

JULIA SYKES

clothes, her fingers shaking with residual fear and anticipation. I allowed her to fumble at my belt, enjoying her desperation for me.

When we were both naked, I scooped her up in my arms and carried her the short distance to the bed. In the few seconds I held her, she pressed sweet kisses against my neck, worshipping my scarred body just as I revered her alabaster perfection.

I laid her beneath me, settling my weight over her to keep her pinned. She didn't squirm or struggle, and that suited my mood. I wanted to take my time with her, not manhandle her.

I skimmed my palms up her arms, guiding them over her head. I cradled her hands in mine, lifting each to my mouth so I could press a tender kiss to the insides of her wrists. She shivered and sighed, softening under me.

Her eyes widened when I picked up my belt from where I'd placed it beside her on the bed. My needy pet hadn't noticed when I'd picked it up along with her.

I looped the leather over my fist and rubbed it against her cheek. She inhaled and let out a low moan as the scent permeated her senses. I'd conditioned her lustful response to the smell of leather. Her nipples pebbled against my chest, and she arched into me, seeking stimulation on her aching buds.

I allowed her to tease herself as I wound the length of my belt around her wrists, binding them together. There wasn't a means to secure her arms in place, so my will would have to be enough to fully restrain her.

I pressed her wrists into the pillows above her head. "Keep them there," I ordered. "I'm going to check you over to make sure you don't have a scratch on you."

"I don't," she protested weakly. "I'm fine."

I rested my palm on her throat, asserting my dominance. "This is for my satisfaction, not yours." My scar tugged on a twisted smile. "But you're welcome to enjoy my examination. Now, be a good girl and stay still. And no more arguing. You're already going to have to wait a long time for your orgasm. If you continue to be a naughty *gatita*, I won't allow you to come at all."

I pressed my thigh between her legs, and her silky arousal wet my skin. She whimpered and rocked against me. I let more of my weight bear down on her, denying her the stimulation she craved.

"No," I said sternly. "You've been very forgetful about who is in charge today. You're mine, Samantha. I control your pleasure. You will obey me." I rubbed my thumb over her artery.

Her lashes fluttered, and she tipped her head to the side, offering me better access to one of the most vulnerable points on her body.

I leaned in and traced the shell of her ear with my tongue. "Good girl." I allowed my praise to roll over her skin, and I felt her flesh pebble beneath my lips when I dropped a kiss on her neck. I sank my teeth into her shoulder, and she cried out. I held her more firmly, refusing to release her until she surrendered.

She stilled beneath me, and I eased my bite, tracing

the little indentations I'd left in her skin with my tongue.

"The only mark you'll bear is mine," I murmured, kissing the spot I'd bitten.

A low humming sound of satisfaction slipped between her lips, and she closed her eyes on a small smile.

"You like being marked and owned, don't you, *cosita*? You love being mine. Everyone will know it when they see this." I brushed my fingertips over the reddened oval left by my teeth. "And you want them to know that you're my sweet little pet, that I'll keep and protect you at any cost. No one gets to touch you but me. You belong to me."

"Yes," she moaned. "I'm yours."

A rumble of savage approval rolled from my chest, and I began to work my way farther down her body, so I could continue branding her with my touch.

I caressed her breasts, nipping at her skin as I rolled her tight nipples between my fingers. She gasped and thrust her chest into my hands, welcoming more sweet torment. She could have lowered her hands and pulled my face closer to her flushed body, but my obedient pet kept her arms stretched over her head, trapped by my command as effectively as iron shackles.

I flicked my tongue over one of her hard buds, teasing until her head thrashed and she whined in need. I eased one hand up her thigh, finding the wet heat between her legs. I petted her pussy, barely brushing my fingers over her swollen lips. In contrast to my gentle touch on her cunt, I bit down on her nipple. She cried out, arching toward me in a futile effort to alleviate the sting. I only allowed her a brief respite in the second it took me to switch over to her other breast, making sure she was thoroughly tortured.

Her hips undulated beneath me, and she rubbed her sex against my hand as I continued to torment her nipples.

When I was satisfied that she'd been adequately punished in that particular area, I skimmed my palm down her stomach, feeling her creamy skin for any signs of injury. I was mostly convinced that Rodríguez hadn't harmed her in any way, but checking for my own peace of mind calmed me.

I settled myself between her legs, grasping her thighs and spreading her wide. I traced the line of her slit with my thumbs, gently examining her sex.

She tried to lift her hips toward my face, and I cupped her cunt in my hand, forcing her back down.

"I have to make sure you're not hurt," I told her, not bothering to hide my cruel pleasure at her frustrating predicament.

"You know I'm not hurt there." She pouted down at me, helpless and completely adorable.

"Hmmm," I mused, nuzzling her inner thigh. "So, you're telling me that your pussy isn't aching?"

"Please." She tried to rotate her hips again, and I increased my grip on her sex, holding her in place while

I delivered a punitive bite to the sensitive skin just beside her outer lips.

I waited for her to shudder and stop defying my control. She stilled, but her muscles quivered with need. My hands eased back to her thighs, gripping firmly as I lowered my face to her wet and waiting cunt.

A low groan left my chest at the first taste of her on my tongue. I explored her slowly and thoroughly, memorizing every contour of her soft body, every little place that made her whimper and jerk beneath me. I'd learned all her erotic triggers a long time ago, but after almost losing her today, I had to take my time savoring her.

I nearly lost myself in her, all rational thoughts leaving my mind as I settled into a more primal head-space. All that existed was her need and my desire to wring pleasure from her body.

I traced my tongue around her clit and rubbed my forefinger over her g-spot. She began to clench around me, on the verge of orgasm.

Suddenly remembering my plan to punish her, I quickly withdrew, denying her just as she reached the peak.

A sob caught in her throat. Before she could wriggle toward me or beg for release, I grabbed her hips and flipped her over, hooking my arm beneath her and drag-ging her onto her knees. She tried to push up and move with me, but I wrapped my hand around her nape and pressed her cheek back against the mattress.

"Stay," I commanded. "I'm not done checking you yet."

I stared down at her for several long seconds, imposing my will. Her lovely blue eyes began to sparkle with the first hint of her pretty tears. My pet had been a fierce lioness today, but it was time to take her in hand and tame her. I stroked the length of her spine, petting her until she softened and practically purred like my sweet kitten.

I released her nape and returned my attention to her pussy, dipping two fingers into her slick arousal before pressing them against her puckered bud.

She tensed, some of her defiance returning. After being so strong and brave in her determination to protect me this afternoon, Samantha was having a hard time fully surrendering control.

"I'm definitely not hurt *there*," she protested breathily.

My free hand cracked against her upper thigh, and I applied pressure to her asshole as she shrieked.

"You don't get to decide where I touch you or how," I reminded her. "Every part of you belongs to me. I want to make sure your body is exactly as responsive as I like it. And you always respond so sweetly when I penetrate your tight little ass." I gripped her hair, forcing her back to arch toward me as I slid my fingers deep inside her. "You know better than to defy your Master, don't you?"

Her entire body shook, and her inner muscles began

JULIA SYKES

to contract around the intrusion of my fingers. I wasn't touching her pussy, and she was on the edge of orgasm just from my invasion of her most intimate area.

I tugged on her hair, commanding her attention. "Answer me."

"I... What did you ask me again?"

She drew in short, panting breaths, and her flushed skin began to glisten with the heat of her arousal. I used my grip on her hair to turn her head to the side, so I could see her face. Her aquamarine eyes slid out of focus, and I had to hold her in my gaze for several heartbeats before she managed to really look at me. When she did finally meet my eye, her lips parted in awe, and she stared at me as though I was the center of her world.

"Master." She whispered my title with reverence.

Something swelled in my chest, something so hot and bright that my body could barely contain it. I had to find release, or it would burn me up.

I gripped my cock and lined myself up with her slick opening. I entered her in one swift, brutal thrust. I'd been taking my time teasing and tormenting her, but this harsh coupling was about satiating my needs now. My desire overwhelmed me. Raw, animal craving took hold of my psyche, and I fucked her at the rough pace that pleased the monster in me.

I kept my fingers deep inside her ass while my free hand sank into her hip, locking her in place so I could claim her in the way I wanted.

She responded to my brutality, coming apart on a sharp cry. Her inner walls gripped me hard, and I hissed with something close to pain at the torturous tightness of her sheath. I gritted my teeth and held back my release. I wasn't nearly done taking my pleasure from her body.

I rode her through her second orgasm, rutting into her until she whimpered and shook beneath me. I braced my hand beneath her belly, holding her upright so I could continue fucking her.

As I began to lose my grip on my own pleasure, I rubbed her clit firmly. She came a third time on a helpless sob, her body responding to my every demand. Her pussy fluttered around me, squeezing my cock with delicious pressure that set my teeth on edge.

I finally released into her with an animal roar, burying myself deep, so my seed would lash inside her belly. I wanted to brand her, to tie her to me in every way possible.

A rough sound of savage satisfaction rumbled from my chest as I kept her captive in my hold, emptying every last drop of my pleasure into her hot cunt.

I'd marked my pet inside and out. Samantha was all mine, and no one would ever take her from me.

CHAPTER 8
SAMANTHA

I tried not to be too conspicuous as I shifted in my seat, easing into a more comfortable position. Valentina and Adrián had a beautiful home with fabulous décor, but their dining chairs weren't nearly cushy enough. I was sore after Andrés' thorough, rough treatment of my body. Even though he'd stroked me in the shower and soothed me, I would feel the aftermath of our harsh lovemaking for a few days, at least.

Even as I tried to surreptitiously shift my weight off my butt, a small smile tugged at my lips. I liked the ache my Master had left deep inside me. I'd managed to hold myself together throughout the scary events that had unfolded earlier today, but I'd needed to feel his strength now that the danger had passed. It reassured me that we were together and safe. It was the sweetest relief to finally let go and cede control to the man I loved and trusted more than anyone else in the world. I could be completely vulnerable with him, and he would always protect me.

"So, that's how I ended up in California." Valentina finished regaling us with the wild story about how she and Adrián had gotten together after years of separation. His hand rested on hers atop the table, and he didn't bother hiding his affection for her. While she spoke, he watched her with something between adoration and hunger.

"I'm glad you're happy." Andrés sounded like he actually meant it, and he'd stopped shooting Adrián threatening glares.

Valentina beamed at him. "I didn't know I could be this happy. I can't believe you're here for the wedding." She turned her dark eyes on me. "Thank you for bringing us back together, Samantha. I know we just met, but we're about to be sisters. I'd be honored if you'd stand with me at the altar tomorrow. Sofia is already my maid of honor, but you could be co-matron of honor."

My throat tightened, and the corners of my eyes burned at a sudden swell of emotion. Until today, Andrés had been the only family member I had left. He was more than enough, but having a sister was a major bonus.

"I'd love that." My words hitched slightly, and I cleared my throat. "But I don't have a dress or anything."

Valentina waved away my concern. "We can order

one tonight, and it'll be delivered in the morning. It'll just take a few minutes to pick one out that you like. I have Sofia's dress in my closet, so you can take a look at it and figure out how you want to coordinate. She's actually about to come sleep over tonight. Will you stay with us?"

Adrián frowned and squeezed her hand. "I don't want you to sleep without me tonight."

She leaned into him and brushed a kiss against his cheek. "We talked about this. It's tradition. The next time you see me, we'll be at the altar."

Adrián's lips thinned, and for a moment, I thought he'd insist on getting his way. I understood his desire to be close to the woman he loved after thinking he'd lost her today.

I glanced over at my own husband. He didn't look too pleased about the prospect of me leaving his bed, either.

"I'd really like to stay with Valentina," I said gently. If I made a demand, he might refuse. Not because he was cruel, but because he'd be hurt that I was rejecting him, and he'd react by shackling me to him so he wouldn't lose me. Even though I belonged to him completely, he was still terrified of being separated from me. He might seem controlling, but his possessive behavior came from a place of vulnerability. I didn't want to cause him any pain.

"Please," Valentina cajoled, appealing to both her fiancé and her brother.

The men sighed, capitulating at the same time. Neither seemed to notice that they mirrored each other; they were too focused on us.

Valentina offered me a small, secret smile. She seemed to understand the commonalities between them, even if they wouldn't admit it to themselves. On the surface, Adrián seemed like a bad guy. He was perfectly content to run his criminal empire, whereas Andrés had easily forsaken his. But in the ways that counted, both men were capable of deep love and devotion. I might not approve of Adrián's nefarious enterprise, but he obviously adored Valentina, and that was good enough for me.

Adrián fixed Andrés with a stony stare. There was no warmth in his hard features, but his pale eyes softened with resignation. "If your wife is staying with Valentina, you're welcome to join Mateo and me for whiskey and cigars this evening."

Andrés inclined his head, accepting the invitation. After a beat of silence, he reluctantly offered an apology. "Sorry for bruising your jaw before your wedding."

Adrián shrugged. "How's your head?"

Andrés didn't have any visible marks on his face, but I remembered his skull cracking against the metal beam in the shed. He hadn't shown any signs of injury, but he probably had a headache.

"Harder than it looks," Andrés replied. "Nothing a little whiskey can't fix."

"Great." Valentina grinned. "Come on, Samantha. Let's go pick out a dress for you."

We all stood, but Adrián grabbed her before she could walk away, catching her wrist and tugging her against him. Her head tipped back, her body instantly softening in offering to him.

I caught Andrés' attention before he could get worked up about seeing their public display of affection. I went up on my toes and pressed a tender kiss to his lips. The distraction was simple and effective. He responded instantly, his hands bracketing my hips to hold me in place as he claimed my mouth. I forced myself to pull away before I became lost in him.

"I'll see you tomorrow," I promised. "I love you."

He caressed my cheek before releasing me. "I love you, too."

Adrián allowed Valentina to extricate herself from his arms, as well. "My bedroom is this way," she told me, walking out of the dining room with one last lingering look at her fiancé.

I followed where she led, making our way through the huge house until we reached the master suite. Similar to the room where Andrés and I had made love, her space was decorated in shades of tan and cream, giving the room a modern, sophisticated vibe. Her style was obviously understated luxury.

She crossed the spacious room and opened a closet door to reveal a massive space that was as big as my bedroom in my old apartment. She quickly sifted through the rows of beautiful dresses and found a pretty, periwinkle blue gown. The floor-length organza seemed to fall too long for her, but she cleared up my confusion.

"This is Sofia's dress for tomorrow," she explained. She eyed the dress, then my figure, assessing my size. "This shade will look lovely with your eyes. And I think the sweetheart neckline will work, but maybe some cap sleeves for you instead of strapless. You and Sofia can coordinate rather than matching exactly. Is that okay?"

"Um, sure," I agreed, a bit baffled by her knowledge of fashion. My style was more casual graphic tees and jeans. Well, it had been before I'd met Andrés. I was mostly naked these days. He made me feel beautiful every day, but it would be nice to wear a pretty dress for him.

"Perfect." Valentina was practically luminous when she smiled. I was very pale and skinny compared to her tanned, voluptuous perfection, but I wasn't plagued by insecurity like I used to be. Andrés loved me exactly as I was, and I didn't need to worry about what anyone else thought. I could appreciate Valentina's beauty without feeling self-conscious about my own appearance.

She led me back into the bedroom, where she retrieved a tablet from atop her vanity. With a few swipes of her well-manicured fingers, she opened a webpage with images of bridesmaids' dresses. She offered the device to me, seeking my approval of her choice.

"It's gorgeous," I agreed.

"It'll look amazing on you. I'll send an email to the boutique owner now to make sure they have it ready for you first thing in the morning. And I'll reach out to my seamstress, too, to make sure she can be on hand for any last-minute adjustments."

"Um, cool. Thanks." I couldn't imagine having a boutique owner's personal email or a seamstress, but Valentina seemed completely at ease with this lifestyle. She was definitely glamorous, and I didn't begrudge her feminine indulgence. If wearing pretty dresses made her happy, more power to her. She would be stunning in yoga pants with no makeup, but she certainly had a figure that practically begged to be adorned.

A knock on the door distracted us.

"That's all done," Valentina announced, setting her tablet aside. "You can come in, Sofia," she called out.

The door opened, and a pretty girl with a mass of glossy black curls stepped inside. She appeared younger that Valentina and me—maybe in her early twenties. Her bright, perfect smile faltered when her deep green gaze fell on me.

"Oh, hey," she said, clearly taken aback by the presence of a stranger in Valentina's bedroom.

"I'm so glad you're here," Valentina said warmly, closing the distance between them and pulling the girl into a firm embrace. When she pulled away, she introduced me. "This is Samantha. She's going to be my sister-in-law tomorrow." She practically buzzed with giddy excitement. "Samantha, this is Sofia. She helped me pick out my classes at UCLA. She was so great making me feel welcome when I moved to California, and now she's stuck with me."

Sofia elbowed her good-naturedly. "It's not exactly a chore hanging out with you, V." She turned to me, and I shifted awkwardly, not sure if I should shake her hand. That felt a little formal when we were about to have a sleepover.

She cleared away my anxiety by pulling me into a familiar hug. "If you're going to be Valentina's sister, then you're mine, too," she declared. "It's really nice to meet you, Samantha."

"You too," I offered, returning her infectious smile. "You can both call me Sam, if you want. That's what all my friends call me."

"Awesome," Sofia approved. "Sam, it is."

Something swelled in my chest. I'd never had many friends, and definitely not female friends. Before I met Andrés, I'd pretty much just had work colleagues and Dex in my life. Sofia and Valentina were welcoming me into their lives with open arms.

I jolted as a loud *pop* pierced the sweet moment.

Valentina giggled. "Sorry. I didn't mean to startle you. We have celebratory bubbles." She hefted a bottle of Champagne that she'd pulled out of her mini-fridge.

"If the men are going to have whiskey, we can indulge in a little wine."

"Oh, none for me, thanks," I said before she could pour a third glass.

She glanced up at me. "Are you sure? We're not going to get drunk or anything. Just a glass or two each. I definitely don't want to be hungover tomorrow."

"Yeah," I replied. "I shouldn't drink any alcohol."

Valentina's jaw dropped. I realized I'd placed my hand on my belly, and I quickly jerked it away.

Shit. I hadn't meant to out myself. Andrés didn't even know I was pregnant yet.

"Oh my god," she gushed. "Oh my god!" She quickly set down the bottle of Champagne and stepped toward me, taking my hands in hers. "I'm going to be an aunt?" Her dark eyes sparkled with emotion, and I realized my own eyes were burning. I blinked, and a joyful tear rolled down my cheek.

"Uh-huh," I said thickly. "But please don't tell Andrés. I'm already going to be in so much trouble with him."

Valentina's brow furrowed. "Won't he be happy that you're pregnant?"

"Oh, yeah." A shaky laugh bubbled up from my chest. "We've been trying for a while now. He'll be ecstatic. But he's going to go all caveman crazy on me when he finds out I knew before we came to rescue you. I, um, didn't want to tell him because I knew he wouldn't let me help him with the op. He needed me to watch his back."

Valentina smiled. "Adrián worries about me, too. I don't know if he would let me help him with something like that at all if he thought he'd be putting me in a remotely dangerous situation. You're very brave."

"I mean, I was with the FBI for years." I shrugged off her praise. "I'm a kickass tech analyst, but a pretty shitty field agent. And Andrés definitely would have left me behind on the safety of our island, but I didn't let him."

Valentina appeared even more impressed. "You're being modest about your skills if you're capable of forcing my brother to do anything. I haven't seen him in a long time, but he grew up big."

"Oh, he's definitely not intimidated by my physical prowess." I laughed. "If I were capable of taking him on in hand-to-hand combat, we probably wouldn't be together right now. I'm not Black Widow or anything like that."

"Black Widow?" Sofia chimed in, her face pinched with confusion.

"You know, from *The Avengers*," I supplied. "I kind of tried to fight Andrés when he first..." I trailed off, blushing. "Well, when we first met. It was pretty embarrassing, actually. I really had no business trying to be a field agent. I'm way more badass with a laptop than my fists."

"You fought him?" Valentina asked, puzzled. "I'm

guessing it's because you were working with the FBI, and Andrés wasn't exactly on the right side of the law back then. Is that right?"

"Um, well. Don't judge or anything, okay? But I figure I shouldn't lie to you, if we're family. Andrés kind of captured me while I was spying on his people. Well, Cristian did," I amended quickly. "Andrés... I mean, he was just trying to keep me safe from Cristian. Things were weird at first. I wasn't like, super happy about being held hostage and whatnot. But we worked through all that, and we really love each other. It's not like a Stockholm Syndrome thing. My friends at the Bureau don't really get it, but what we have is real. Andrés saved me. He stood up to Cristian for me and left everything behind so we could be safe together. He's the best thing that ever happened to me."

Valentina squeezed my hand. "I understand."

"Okay, good. I really don't want to mess up your relationship with Andrés by telling you this. He's been through a lot, but he's a good man. The best."

"I really do get it. Better than anyone. I feel the same way about Adrián."

I breathed a sigh of relief. I became aware of Sofia's tense presence. I glanced over at her and noticed she'd drained half her glass of Champagne.

"Oh," I said, my cheeks heating. "Sorry if I made you uncomfortable, Sofia. I know that's not um, a normal love story."

"Totally okay," she reassured me, but she tipped

back her glass and swallowed the rest of her Champagne.

"You're allowed to like Mateo," Valentina encouraged the girl gently. "I know things are complicated between the two of you, but I can tell you care about him."

Sofia's curls bounced as she jerked her head to the side. She poured another glass of Champagne. "It's been a weird day," she said. "I'd rather not talk about Mateo right now."

"You know he practically worships the ground you walk on," Valentina pressed.

"Well, I wish he'd go worship the ground somewhere else," she snapped. "I'm sick of him watching me all the time. I'm sick of men trying to control me. This isn't how my life is supposed to go." She sucked in a deep breath and took another gulp of bubbly. "Anyway," she waved away her anger. "This is your night, Valentina. We don't need to discuss my drama. Let's talk about the wedding. Is everything running smoothly? Do you need me to go into full bitch mode on anyone? Because I totally will. You just sit back and relax, and I'll handle anyone who might annoy you."

Valentina laughed, dispelling the odd tension. I didn't know what was going on between Mateo and Sofia, but it wasn't any of my business. He'd seemed anxious to get back to her earlier this afternoon, but she made it sound like she didn't want him around her at all. If talking about the situation upset the girl, I wouldn't press. She was right; this was Valentina's night, and it wasn't the right time for drama.

"You couldn't be a bitch if you tried," she told Sofia.

"Trust me, I have a lot of bitch energy going on inside me right now. I'm more than happy to unleash it on the person of your choosing."

"Everything's going perfectly," Valentina reassured her friend. "No need to do any damage control, but thank you for offering." She let out a happy sigh and grinned at me. "I didn't know it could be this perfect, actually. You brought Andrés back to me, and I'm getting a sister, too. And a little niece or nephew," she added, practically glowing with joy. "My family is bigger than ever."

"Mine too," I said hoarsely, my eyes stinging again.

I could hardly believe how lucky I was that Andrés had come into my life. Who would have thought that being kidnapped by a drug lord could have such an awesome outcome? Our happily-ever-after might be unconventional, but that didn't make it any less perfect.

CHAPTER 9
ANDRÉS

"**A**re you ready?" I asked on a rasp. Valentina was radiant in her white lace wedding gown. She looked so different from the young girl I'd known, but the bright spark in her eyes and her broad smile were the same. Even though I knew she must have endured horrific treatment during the years that had separated us, she was still capable of expressing pure joy. Adrián brought her this happiness. I supposed that meant I truly couldn't hate him.

She placed her hand on my forearm, squeezing gently. "More than ready, big brother."

She took a deep breath and turned to face forward. Her full attention focused on the chapel doors, which hid the man she loved from her sight.

I nodded at the two waiting ushers, and they opened the doors to admit us. Valentina took a step forward, guiding me along in her eagerness to reach Adrián. I was symbolically giving my blessing, but she was definitely the one walking me down the aisle. I wouldn't have been able to hold her back even if I wanted to.

She might be fully focused on Adrián, but my gaze riveted on Samantha. I faltered a step, forgetting how to breathe. I was so accustomed to seeing her wearing casual clothes or nothing at all. My wife was perfect without a stitch of clothing or hint of makeup, but she was particularly stunning in her gauzy, pale blue gown. Her alabaster skin glowed, her wide, entrancing eyes sparkling. She appeared ethereal, too beautiful to be real.

She watched me with an open hunger that matched my own. She looked at me as though I was someone to be revered, not a scarred monster.

Suddenly, I was at the altar. I took a step toward Samantha, momentarily forgetting my role in my all-consuming obsession with her. She shook her head with a rueful smile, tipping her bouquet in the direction of the pew behind me. It was time for me to leave Valentina with her husband and take my place among the other seated guests.

I placed Valentina's hand in Adrián's, shooting the man one last warning glare. If he ever hurt my sister, he was a dead man.

He didn't notice my flash of animosity. His full attention was fixed on Valentina, his pale eyes sparking with awe. I didn't appreciate the way he looked as though he wanted to devour her with his possessive gaze, but her beatific expression was enough to make me step away, resigning myself to their union.

I released Valentina's hand and took my reserved seat. In my sweeping assessment of the happy scene unfolding before me, I noticed Mateo standing at Adrián's side, taking his place as best man. He wasn't watching the bride and groom. Instead, he stared at Sofia.

I glanced over at her. She resolutely kept her eyes on Valentina, the slight tension in her willowy frame indicating that she was well aware of Mateo's intense attention, and she didn't appreciate it.

I shrugged off their odd behavior. They didn't really matter to me, even though Mateo seemed nice enough after we'd shared a few drinks last night. It wasn't as though we were going to be friends, and I simply appreciated him as extra, enormous security around my little sister. What he did with Sofia was his business, not mine.

My gaze fell on Samantha again, and I didn't even try to resist staring. I was peripherally aware that Valentina and Adrián were exchanging vows, but the ceremony passed by in a blur. Samantha mostly focused on the happy couple, but she could clearly feel the sharpness of my eyes on her. Every time she looked at me, her cheeks colored with the pretty pink blush I loved so much. She shifted on her feet a few times, and I wondered if she was still aching inside from when I'd fucked her yesterday. I liked the idea of her feeling me, even though I couldn't touch her at the moment.

She tipped her head to the side, and her shining copper hair slipped behind her shoulder, revealing the mark I'd left on her with my teeth. She hadn't covered the bruise with foundation for the sake of appearances. She didn't care what the strangers around us thought; she wore my brand with pride.

My mouth watered, my gut tightening. I couldn't wait to get my wife back to the privacy of our home so I could mark her flesh in other ways. I hadn't reddened her ass with my whip in far too long. I wasn't feeling particularly sadistic, just possessive. That was as good a reason as any to torment her until she wept in desperation for me. I'd make sure to reward her with more pleasure than she could bear.

The ceremony ended with an eruption of clapping and cheers as Adrián swept Valentina up in a fierce kiss. Pretty tears glistened on Samantha's cheeks as she watched them process back down the aisle, Valentina practically bouncing with happiness as Adrián held her hand tightly in his.

Mateo took Sofia's arm and led her out of the church, and I immediately stood to go to my wife. We'd never had a public ceremony for our own wedding, and I settled into the joy of the moment. As I led Samantha down the aisle, I held her close to my side. She laughed in delight, catching onto the levity of the cheering crowd.

"Are you disappointed we didn't have a big wedding like this?" I murmured.

She looked up at me, her gorgeous eyes wide and earnest. "Of course not. Our wedding was perfect. We didn't need a bunch of people there. I don't need their validation to know you're mine."

A low chuckle rumbled from my chest. "That's my fierce *gatita*."

Her grin took on a saucy twist. "Well, you are mine, Andrés. My husband. My Master."

She was teasing and tempting me when she knew I couldn't do anything about it in public. She was fully aware of the effect her words had on me. My pet had given me all the excuse I needed to redden her ass as soon as we got home.

❧

SAMANTHA MUST HAVE SENSED MY MOOD, BECAUSE HER tension grew the farther we got from LA and the closer we got to our island home. I allowed her to stew in it, enjoying her trepidation. I didn't take my hands off her during the whole flight. As soon as we'd left the wedding reception, I started toying with her. She'd dared to tease me, but I was much more patient than she was. She might get a little thrill out of provoking me, but I could revel in tormenting her for hours without getting bored.

By the time we stepped into the private haven of

our house, she was wound so tightly that her body was practically vibrating in my hold.

I brushed my thumb over her lush lips, drawing a soft gasp from her. "What's the matter, *cosita?*" I drawled. "Is something frustrating you?"

She swallowed. "I, um... No. I'm not frustrated. Not exactly."

"Hmmm," I mused, trailing my fingers down her throat before lightly pressing on the tender mark on her shoulder. "Tell me what's bothering you, *sirenita*," I commanded, anticipating her plea for release.

"I'm pregnant," she blurted out, like it was an admission of guilt.

Shock tore through my body, obliterating any ability to ponder over her strange tone. Several seconds of silence passed while my brain stalled out.

"Andrés?" she squeaked. "I'm sorry, okay? Don't be mad."

"Why would I be mad?" I asked, my voice rough with emotion. Unadulterated joy surged, and I barked out a laugh as I grabbed my wife and spun her around. For a few moments, I held her against me with all my strength.

I released her abruptly, setting her back down on her feet. I anxiously ran my hands over her body to soothe away any damage I might have inflicted. "Did I hurt you?" I asked. "I didn't mean to hold you so tight."

She beamed up at me, cupping my cheek in her hand to reassure me. "I'm fine. I'm not made of glass all of a sudden. You can hug me as tight as you want. I like it." She licked her lips, uncertainty flickering in her lovely eyes. "So, um, I want you to remember how happy you are right now. And, you know, I want you to hug me and all that, but maybe think about the whole taking it easy on me thing, okay?"

I gripped her chin, tilting her head back so I could study her face. "Tell me what you've done, Samantha."

"Nothing!" she said quickly. "Well, it's about what I *didn't* do. I kind of found out I was pregnant last week. I took the test before I told you that I'd found Valentina. Because, you know, you wouldn't have let me help you if you'd known about the baby. And I couldn't let you go in alone. Everything worked out fine, anyway. So, it's all good. Happy endings for everyone. Because you're happy, right? I'm happy. Don't be mad. Please?"

I kept my firm hold on her chin, but I stroked my free hand through her hair, soothing her worry. "I've never been happier in my life," I swore. "You've given me everything, Samantha. More than I ever could have dreamed of. I have my sister back. I have you. And now, we're starting our own family."

I loved her so much, I could hardly contain the heat in my chest. Samantha was my miracle, and I would never let go of something so precious. I coveted her and guarded her as closely as the most valuable treasure in the world, but I didn't feel any shame over my posses-siveness. Samantha was blissfully happy in my care, and she gave herself to me willingly. I didn't have to cage her to ensure she was forever mine.

"So, we're all good?" she asked tentatively. "You're not going to punish me for keeping this from you?"

My scar drew tight on a cruel smile. "I didn't say that, *gatita*."

She trembled against me, but she didn't try to pull away. "I figured I had it coming," she admitted. "But it was worth it. I couldn't let you go to LA alone."

I wrapped my hand around her nape, applying firm pressure. "Naughty little pet," I chided. "You knew you were doing something wrong, but you chose to displease your Master anyway."

She lifted her chin. "Yep. And I'd do it again. I wouldn't ever let anyone hurt you, Andrés."

"I won't let anyone hurt you, either, *cosita*." I placed my hand on her belly. "I'll never let anyone threaten our family."

She offered a weak smile. "Then I guess it's a good thing we have a scary drug lord as a brother-in-law. It's nice to know we have backup if we ever do get in a tight situation. So, this all worked out great, right? Like, I really should be off the hook. Because we're even better off than we were before."

"Oh no, pet." I smirked. "You can't talk your way out of this one. You knew you would be punished when you made your decision. And you don't really want to go unpunished, do you?"

"No," she whispered, the truth slipping from her

easily. Samantha liked when I disciplined her. And she'd more than earned the consequences for her actions this time.

I pressed a kiss to her forehead. "Good girl. Now, I think you've let your mouth run away with you far too much over the last few days. I'm sure that's been very exhausting for you. You've been practically begging me to gag you."

Her cheeks flushed scarlet, and her pupils dilated.

"That's what I thought," I said with arrogant satisfaction. I stroked my fingers through her hair, watching with fascination as she softened into her submissive headspace. "What else should I do to you, naughty pet? What punishment do you think you've earned?"

"Whatever you want, Master," she breathed.

Her response was perfect. *She* was perfect. Somehow, Samantha managed to be my sweet, obedient pet and my clever, fiercely independent wife. She might call me *Master*, but we truly were partners in life. We were family.

I'd always craved control and demanded the subservience of those around me, but I would be completely devoted to my family. I'd do anything to protect the people I loved and ensure their happiness.

And I'd start right now by seeing to Samantha's needs. My pet was going to love every second of her devious punishment. I wouldn't have it any other way.

The End

ALSO BY JULIA SYKES

The Captive Series

Sweet Captivity

Claiming My Sweet Captive

Stealing Beauty

Captive Ever After

Pretty Hostage

Kingpin's Property

The Impossible Series

Impossible

Savior

Rogue

Knight

Mentor

Master

King

A Decadent Christmas (An Impossible Series Christmas Special)

Czar

Crusader

Prey (An Impossible Series Short Story)

Highlander

Decadent Knights (An Impossible Series Short Story)

Centurion

Dex

Hero

Wedding Knight (An Impossible Series Short Story)

Valentines at Dusk (An Impossible Series Short Story)

Nice & Naughty (An Impossible Series Christmas Special)

Dark Lessons

RENEGADE: The Complete Series

The Daddy and The Dom

The Dark Grove Plantation Series

Holden

Brandon

Damien

Made in the USA
Middletown, DE
02 December 2020